In today's top movies and TV shows, the side-kick characters are getting the most attention. Catch up with the talented young actors who are stealing the spotlight!

★ **Seth Green,** who shined in supporting roles on *Buffy the Vampire Slayer* and in the *Austin Powers* movies, and is now one of the hottest names in young Hollywood.

★ **Ashton Kutcher,** whose scene-stealing portrayal of dim-bulb Kelso on *That 70s Show* has propelled him into films, including *Down to You* and *Texas Rangers*.

★ **Scott Speedman,** who lured *Felicity* to New York before taking over Brad Pitt's role in the hit movie *Duets* with Gwyneth Paltrow.

★ **Plus many more!**

With color photos and the ultimate second-banana trivia quiz, this book has all the info on the hot young stars who are . . .

Second to None

Look for other celebrity biographies from Archway Paperbacks

second to none:

superstars on the rise

nancy krulik

AN ARCHWAY PAPERBACK
Published by POCKET BOOKS
New York London Toronto Sydney Singapore

AN ARCHWAY PAPERBACK Original

An Archway Paperback published by
POCKET BOOKS, a division of Simon & Schuster Inc.
1230 Avenue of the Americas, New York, NY 10020

ISBN: 0-671-78533-8

First Archway Paperback printing April 2000

10 9 8 7 6 5 4 3 2 1

AN ARCHWAY PAPERBACK and colophon are
registered trademarks of Simon & Schuster Inc.

Front cover photos by (clockwise from top): Globe Photos, Inc.;
Walter McBride / Retna; Steve Granitz / Retna

Printed in the U.S.A.

IL 4+

For my parents,
Gladys and Steve,
who are truly second to none

Contents

Contents

Introduction
Starring . . . The Sidekicks

There are no small parts, only small actors.

How many times have you heard that one? It's the battle cry of performers with few lines, little screen time, and empty wallets. But the truth is, the acting biz hasn't always worked that way. In fact, for decades, Hollywood has applauded only the leading players—making sure they got all the press and publicity, and filling their bank accounts with lots and lots of cold hard cash. That kind of attitude has basically left all the other actors fighting for whatever scraps are left over.

But today there's a revolution going on in the entertainment world. The supporting players are mad, and they're not gonna take it anymore! The sidekicks are rising up and taking over. And the fans couldn't be happier.

1

Sidekicks are the characters who add humor to tense moments, and who give the leading actors someone to talk to. Ever since there have been actors and writers, there have been sidekicks. You'll find them in Shakespeare's plays as well as in today's hit sitcoms and dramas. You know the type—the best friend, the pesky little brother, the wacky aunt, or the coworker with the quick quips. Surprisingly, the sidekick roles are often the best-written parts, since, unlike leading actors, sidekicks don't have to be drop-dead gorgeous all the time (although, as the fourteen guys in this book prove, they certainly can be). That means the second bananas are open for doing intense physical comedy that leaves them with pie on their face (think Kel Mitchell), or for snapping out nasty comebacks that are memorable if not necessarily likable (think Seth Green's *Austin Powers* character, Scott Evil). And you gotta admit, that kind of stuff is a lot more fun than standing still for your 185th close-up!

Where would movies, TV, and theater be without sidekicks? Pretty much nowhere. Holy second banana, Batman! Can you picture the caped crusader without his sidekick, Robin? And where would *I Love Lucy*'s Ricky and Lucy Ricardo be without their pals, Fred and Ethel Mertz? How about Luke Skywalker without Han Solo?

The truth is, it's the sidekicks that give movies and TV shows their bite. And for the first time, the fans are starting to discover who the *real* stars are. More and more Web sites dedicated to second bananas are popping up. (In fact, in the case of *Dawson's Creek*, there are more fan sites dedicated to Joshua Jackson, who plays Dawson's best friend, Pacey, than there are for James Van Der Beek, who plays Dawson.)

Sidekicks are taking home the top prizes at teen celebrity contests as well. When the E! cable network took a vote to determine who the hottest young actors in Hollywood were, the number one choice among teens was none other than super sidekick Seth Green. And when *Seventeen* magazine sponsored the Teen Choice Awards, it was *Dawson's Creek*'s Joshua Jackson who took home the choice male TV actor prize. Seems these days girls are going for humor and intelligence, as well as all-around cuteness, when it comes to choosing their top guys.

The fourteen guys in this book have made a career of being the supporting players to the stars—and gained fame and fortune in the process. As far as the fans are concerned, these sidekicks are truly second to none!

Nicholas Brendon
The Comic Relief

Look. Over there. Do you see that tall guy with the brown hair and the dreamy hazel eyes? Isn't that Nicholas Brendon, the guy who plays Xander on *Buffy the Vampire Slayer*?

Don't be so sure. The next time you're hanging out at the local mall and you think you've been lucky enough to come face-to-face with Nicholas Brendon, think twice before asking for his autograph. Sure, it might be Nicky (as his friends and family call him)—but it could be his identical twin brother, Kelly.

That's right! There are two guys walking around out there who are both equally gorgeous. And that sometimes causes troubles for Nicky's bro.

"There was this one time we were driving to

Yosemite, and we had driven separately, and a busload of teenage girls recognized [Kelly] and asked him for his autograph," Nicky recalls. "He said, 'No, that's my twin brother.' They didn't believe him and started throwing french fries at him."

But according to the brothers, that's a small price to pay for having the incredibly special relationship that only twins can have.

"He's been my best friend ever since we shared my mom's belly," Nicky swears.

Nicky is the younger of the two twins, if only by three minutes. You wouldn't think such a minuscule age difference would matter much, but it did to Nicky. Especially during the twins' annual birthday celebration.

"[Kelly] always got his cake and happy birthday song first. Mine would come just minutes later, but by that time our friends were already eating his cake. They weren't into my cake any more."

Poor kid. Still, Nicky is the first to say that having a twin brother is pretty great. "We were never lonely," he says of his relationship with Kelly. "You always had a person to play with. You always had someone to confide in; someone to talk to. And someone just to beat up."

Oh, did we forget to mention that Nicky has a real sarcastic side to him?

Even though Nicky and Kelly may look alike,

Nancy Krulik

they are two completely different human beings, with their own likes and dislikes. But that doesn't come as a surprise to Nicky's millions of fans. They've known all along that there's only one Nicholas Brendon!

A Vampire Slayer Grows Up

Nicky grew up in Granada Hills, in the San Fernando Valley area of Los Angeles. During his early life, he shared his house with his parents, Kelly, and his two younger brothers, Christian and Kyle. He had a pretty normal childhood—playing Little League ball, getting decent (if not stellar) grades, and every now and then pulling the old "identical twin switch" to try and get out of taking an especially difficult test. (Inevitably, he and Kelly got caught, but, hey, you can't blame the kids for trying.)

Although Nicky's mom is a theatrical talent agent, acting never crossed his mind when he was a kid. Nicky had a very different dream. He wanted to play pro baseball. And not just for any team. Nicky wanted to play for the Los Angeles Dodgers.

"I love the Dodgers," Nicky explains. "I was dead serious about playing for the Los Angeles Dodgers."

And Nicky pursued that dream with all the power he had in him. Throughout his childhood, he played competitive ball, in Little League and on his school teams. Nicky was good enough to score a starting position as a right fielder on his Chatsworth High School team by his junior year. That was no small feat, considering Nicky's high school baseball team was ranked number one in the country.

Baseball was Nicky's saving grace in high school. Nothing else seemed to be going for him at the time. Although Kelly entered high school with an inner confidence, Nicky couldn't seem to muster the courage to speak to many people, especially girls.

"You think Xander hates high school? Well, I redefined teen angst," Nicky told *Teen People* magazine. "While Kelly went to parties and out on dates, I remained girlfriendless for all four years, and had acne, braces, and, worst of all, a stutter."

What Now?

If his high school life was difficult, Nicky soon learned that life after graduation was not going to get much better. While playing for his college baseball team, Nicky fractured his elbow, and his lifelong dream of playing for the Dodgers was gone forever. He was very upset, naturally, and he found himself unable to focus on his studies. His grades dropped. And then, just when he figured life couldn't get any worse, something he never thought possible happened. His parents split up.

Ironically, Nicky says that that last straw was what drove him toward performing. He needed to do something that made him feel good about himself. And the only way he could do that was to make *other* people happy—by entertaining them.

By the time he entered college, Nicky was much more attractive than he had been during his high school days. His braces had left behind perfectly straight pearly whites, and his skin had cleared up. Since he'd been an athlete for so long, his bod was totally toned. He definitely had the looks that casting directors go for.

But Nicky had a big problem. He still had that stammer. Nicky has never spoken publicly about why he thought he developed the speech impediment, saying only that "it's something that happened when I was a child that triggered it. Later on in my career, I might talk about it, but right now, I won't."

Rather than focus on *why* he stuttered, Nicky decided to focus on beating the problem. He spent hours in his room tackling tongue twisters and practicing slowing down his speech. Today, the stammer is rarely a problem for him.

Once he had his voice under control, Nicky

asked his mother to help him go out on auditions. Because of her theatrical connections, Nicky's mom was able to get him in the right doors. But getting in the door won't get you the job. It was up to Nicky to prove to the casting directors that he was more than just a pretty face.

Nicky's first acting job was a Clearasil commercial. Having suffered with acne for most of his teen life, Nicky was perfect for the part. After all, who knew better about trying to rid your face of those nasty zits?

Nicky went on to do a few more commercials, for Burger King and Sprite. He also took on roles with some regional theater companies, including parts in shows like *The Further Adventures of Tom Sawyer* and *My Own Private Hollywood*. The experience was great, but the pay was lousy. So Nicky started working on the other side of the camera, as a production assistant on the TV sitcom *Dave's World*.

But if the truth be told, Nicky was not exactly a great p.a. on the set of *Dave's World*. Eventually, he was fired from the job—only to be brought back to the set a few weeks later, as a guest star on the show. The producers obviously were more impressed with Nicky's looks and acting ability than they were with his ability to move scenery and check for props.

After his appearance on *Dave's World*, Nicky

scored a small role in the movie *Children of the Corn III* and bit parts on TV shows like *The Young and the Restless* and *Married . . . with Children*. But those parts were few and far between, and Nicky finally took on the part most out-of-work L.A. actors eventually have to take—a waiter in a local restaurant.

It was while he was waiting tables that Nicky heard about an audition for a project called *Buffy the Vampire Slayer*, which was to be produced by screenwriter Joss Whedon (*Toy Story, Twister*).

Joss had a great attachment to *Buffy the Vampire Slayer*. In 1992, he had written a movie of the same name. The film, a teen comedy that starred *Beverly Hills 90210*'s Luke Perry, was a total bomb at the box office. Joss was so disappointed that he decided to go back and remake the story of a teenage girl who discovers she is the one chosen to fight evil on earth. But this time, Joss was making the property into a series for television. And this time, he was going to do it right.

Instead of making the TV *Buffy* a comedy, Joss went straight for the horror vein (pun totally intended!). He wanted to scare teenagers—big time. But he also needed a character that would lighten things up from time to time by adding the comic relief. That's where the role of Alexander (Xander) Harris came in.

"When I first went in for [the audition], it wasn't even a pilot. It was a presentation," Nicky recalls of his initial meeting with the show's casting agents.

That meeting was the beginning of a whirlwind of events that would eventually change Nicky's life forever.

"It took me a matter of five days," Nicky says of the audition process for the role of Xander. "Four auditions and five days. It was quick. I had come in toward the end, and I think they were just horribly desperate."

Now, that's something the fans would find hard to believe. In fact, it's hard to imagine anyone being more perfect for the role of Buffy's goofy, wacky, vampire-slaying sidekick.

Fans and critics agree that Nicky has managed to make Xander a very true-life character. Maybe that's because there's a lot of Nicky in Xander. Xander shares Nicky's innate sarcastic charm, as well as his desire to be there to help out his friends. He also shares some of Nicky's high school insecurities, especially where women are concerned.

But Nicky says he doesn't get all of his inspiration for the character from his own life. In fact, he believes that Xander's personality has some more "animated" roots.

"Xander is both Shaggy and Scooby-Doo wrapped into one neat little package," he says, comparing his character to the cartoon crime fighters.

But in a show that is often filled with blood-sucking vampires, werewolves, mummies, and all forms of evil beings, sometimes it takes a little cartoonlike buffoonery to keep things from going over the top.

Life on the Set

Today, the cast of *Buffy the Vampire Slayer* is about as tight as any group of coworkers can possibly be. It's hard to believe that the gang didn't meet until production began on the show in September of 1996.

"The WB put six strangers together and sent us off for four months of rehearsing and training, and it worked," Nicky told *Teen People* of the early days on the *Buffy* set. "We all got along and it translated into a successful show."

That's an understatement. Today, Buffy is the highest-rated show among preteen and teenage girls—its intended audience. And the gang is so much like a family that Nicky says he would go out of the way to protect them, just as he would for any of his brothers.

"We're like brothers and sisters," he says of his friendship with cast members Sarah Michelle Gellar (Buffy), Alyson Hannigan (Willow), Charisma Carpenter (Cordelia, now star-

ring on *Angel,* the Buffy spin-off), Seth Green
(Oz), and David Boreanaz (Angel, now starring
in *Angel*). "We all live for each other and would
probably die for each other."

What Does the Future Hold?

Although shooting an hour-long drama takes up
much of his free time, Nicky has managed to
take his career in several new and exciting di-
rections. He's got major roles in two hot up-
coming flicks. The first, *Piñata,* is the story of
an ancient Central American village's desperate
attempt to rid itself of a dark force that is released through a piñata. The second is called
Psycho Beach Party. It's a murder mystery about
a girl with multiple personalities who hangs out
with a group of surfers. There's also been talk of
casting Nicky in the role of Spider-Man in the
big-screen movie based on the comic-book
character. So far, there's no truth to that rumor,
although Joss Whedon is one of the producers
jockeying to bring Spidey's story to the silver
screen.

Nicky is currently living in a Spanish-style
duplex in the Hollywood hills. He shares his
fancy new digs with his brother Kelly. Kelly has
gone into acting, too, and, according to Nicky,
his brother is making a really positive impression on agents out in L.A. So before long, there

may be two gorgeous Brendon brothers collecting fan mail. (Just don't try to contact Nicky via E-mail. He doesn't even own a computer.)

As for his romantic life, Nicky is making major strides. He's finally got himself a steady girl, an actress and a model, whom he met at a softball game. While Nicky prefers to keep the details private, he does say that "she's probably the most amazing person I know. I actually met her before I got the show. She's inspired me and she's coached me. Everything just kind of fell into place."

We guess you could say that, these days, Nicky is really taking a *bite* out of life!

Fast Facts

Full Name: Nicholas Brendon Shultz
Nickname: Nicky
Birthday: April 12, 1971
Astrological sign: Aries
Parents: Bob and Kathy
Brothers: Kelly, Christian, and Kyle
Favorite actors: Jack Lemmon, Jim Carrey
Favorite movie: *Some Like It Hot*
Favorite TV shows: *The Simpsons*, *Seinfeld*, *The X-Files*
Favorite musicians: Frank Sinatra, Louis Armstrong, Beck, Nerf Herder
Favorite color: Blue
Favorite childhood book: *The Giving Tree* by Shel Silverstein

Scott Foley
Resident Dork or Darling?

"I'd love to guest star on *Leave It to Beaver*," Scott Foley says, describing his biggest career fantasy. "It's my all-time favorite show. I want to redo that episode where Beaver gets his head caught in the gate. I could play that guy who gets his head unstuck."

Leave It to Beaver? Could remaking a 1950s sitcom that can only be called one of the dorkiest shows of all time really be the dream job for an actor recently named one of *TV Guide*'s sixteen sexiest stars?

You betcha!

Scott Foley isn't the kind of actor to be taken in by all the Hollywood hype, or by the women who follow him around the local mall, drooling over his six-foot-two-inch muscular frame and his dazzling sea-green eyes. He knows what kind of person he really is deep down.

"I know, I'm a huge dork," he admits.

A dork, maybe, but he's also one of the hottest young actors on the entertainment scene. And that's a very unusual feeling for Scott, because for more than seven years he hung around Hollywood, desperately waiting for someone to give him his big break. But instead of being called on to act in the next big thang, Scott found himself working the night shift at a Mrs. Fields cookie store, managing local restaurants, and selling car insurance—even though he didn't have enough money for a car.

But of course, that's all changed now. Suddenly this twenty-seven-year-old, dark-haired honey is the hottest resident assistant on the airwaves—*Felicity's* Noel Crane. And life couldn't be better.

" 'Amazing' is my favorite word of late," he recently told a chat audience. "People have asked me recently, 'How are you doing?' and I say, 'Amazingly well.' "

Once Upon a Time . . .

The "amazing" Scott Foley was born on July 15, 1972, in Kansas City, Kansas. As he was growing up, Scott must have found himself saying,

"I don't think we're in Kansas anymore" a lot more times than *The Wizard of Oz*'s Dorothy ever did. That's because Scott had lived all over the world before he even reached the age of fourteen. His father was an international banker whose work took the family to places as far from Kansas as Sydney, Australia, and Tokyo, Japan.

By the time Scott was nine, he knew that the only thing he ever wanted to do was perform. This revelation came when he was in the fourth grade and sang "I'll Do Anything" from the musical *Oliver* in a school play. From that moment on, he knew he was going to be an actor. And, as it turned out, his love of acting helped keep him happy as his family moved from place to place. It was the one constant in an ever-changing lifestyle.

"We moved around a lot when I was younger—Australia, Japan, Hawaii, the mainland," he recently told a chat audience. "But [acting] was always something I could do no matter where I went. I couldn't play football in Australia; I had to play rugby. But acting was always there."

In fact, Scott was so single-minded about his career choice that he never even considered studying something else to fall back on. When the Foley family finally settled down in Saint Louis, Missouri, Scott began taking part in regional theater. He focused all his efforts on his acting, and didn't put a whole lot of effort into his high school education. "I went to three different high schools, and was a troublemaker in all of them," he admitted in *ym* magazine.

By his senior year in high school, while the other kids in school were studying for their college entrance exams, Scott was studying monologues. He never took his SATs, and—here's a real shocker—he never went to college! He's just playing Noel on instinct.

In June of 1992, right after his high school graduation, Scott bought a one-way plane ticket to Los Angeles. He didn't have a job, an agent, or any real money in his pocket. In fact, he didn't even have a map of California. The only place he'd ever really heard of was Burbank, where *The Tonight Show* is taped.

California, Here He Comes!

Since Burbank was the only place Scott could think of when he got off the plane at LAX, he headed over there and found himself a place to live. Suffice it to say that Scott's new bachelor pad was not exactly fit for a star. "I was nineteen, living in Hollywood, in a single room," he admits. And while his dreams were still grand, Scott learned quickly that you need a lot more than big dreams and talent to become an actor in California.

"It was tough," he recalled to a reporter for the Scripps Howard News Service. "It takes money to get started. You need pictures, résumés printed up, a car to get to auditions. For me, it was a reality check. You just don't just move to L.A. and become an actor."

For the next seven years, Scott scrambled to pay the bills by taking on any kind of work he could get. But after a while, selling car insurance, stocking nursing supplies at a local hospital, and waiting on irritable customers took its toll on Scott. He admits he began to wonder just what made him think he could be an actor, anyway.

"I just decided I didn't want to be an actor anymore," he says of what was probably the most depressing time in his life. So he used some money he'd received as a birthday present from a relative and moved to the Virgin Islands. He hung out on the beaches there until his cash ran out. Then he called his dad and asked him to send him the plane fare home—to Saint Louis, where the family was living at the time.

Scott's ever-supportive father sent him plane fare, all right, but not to Saint Louis. "He said he was flying me back to Los Angeles," Scott recalls.

Scott was so buoyed by his dad's support that he took his father up on his offer and returned to Los Angeles. But when he got there, things looked bleaker than ever before. He couldn't even find a job as a waiter, and was forced to sell cookies at a local Mrs. Fields. For three months, he worked at night and wandered the streets by day, just killing time and going on auditions.

And then in 1998, after seven years of what can only be called bad luck, Scott went on a tryout that would change his life. He auditioned for a talent agent who saw something special in the way Scott could get to the heart of a character and make him seem real. The agent signed Scott immediately, and began sending him out on calls to casting agents.

Scott's first few auditions went well, but not well enough. He would often be called back, but he never seemed to get the role. "I almost got a Mentos commercial where the guy rolls in the wet paint," he remembers. "If you watch, there's a striking resemblance to me."

Eventually, however, he scored his first on-screen role—as a valet named Matt in a made-for-TV movie called *Crowned and Dangerous*, which starred Yasmine Bleeth. The part wasn't very big, but just being on-screen with the gorgeous Yasmine gave Scott bragging rights with his friends. It also restored his confidence.

Scott went on to a guest role on the TV sitcom *Step by Step*, and to score small roles in two more made-for-TV movies: *Someone to*

Love Me, which starred Wonder Woman herself, Lynda Carter, and *Forever Love*, in which Scott shared the stage with country music legend Reba McEntire.

"I could not stop staring at her," Scott says of his time on the soundstage with Reba. "She is the cutest thing in the world, and so professional."

Scott's next acting job was the one that finally helped him break through the Hollywood barriers. He took on the part of high school football hero Cliff Elliott in the new WB teen drama *Dawson's Creek*.

Stealing the Girl, and the Screen, from Dawson

Scott flew down to Wilmington, North Carolina, to take on the role of Cliff in the summer of 1997. Although he was able to step into Cliff's skin without any difficulty, making the twenty-five-year-old Scott look like a sixteen-year-old high school student was the job of the show's makeup department.

"I had to sit through a lot of hours of makeup to play a sixteen-year-old," he recalls.

Still, Scott was convincing in the role—so convincing, in fact, that although he was originally scheduled to appear only in two episodes of *Dawson's Creek*, he signed on for an additional three shows. His story line—in which he stole Jen's heart away from Dawson—made him the guy fans most loved to hate on the show.

Although Scott was older than most of the cast of *Dawson's Creek*, he became quite friendly with them, acting as a sort of surrogate big brother for the fledgling actors. And even after he left the set, Scott remained close with two of the actors, Joshua Jackson and Katie Holmes.

"Katie is still one of my closest friends," he told a chat audience recently. "I still speak to her probably three times a day."

Joshua Jackson told *Entertainment Weekly* that his buddy Scott is "shamefacedly white bread . . . a walking, talking Gap ad. But he has this latent charm, just like Noel; instead of crossing the line into the saccharine zone, it's almost like he's winking at you."

Well, producers J.J. Abrams and Matt Reeves must have a real taste for white bread, because in 1998 they cast Scott for not one but *two* roles on their new television series, *Felicity*.

Noel or Ben—the Producers Must Choose

When Scott Foley auditioned for a role on *Felicity*, he tried out for two parts—Ben, the guy Felicity travels to New York to be near; and Noel, the resident assistant in Felicity's dormitory at the fictional University of New York. J.J. and Matt loved him in both parts.

But the producers felt that it would be easier for them to cast the slightly nerdy role of Noel than it would be for them to find just the right actor to portray the complicated, confused, darker role of Ben. Ben was an athlete, similar to the role of Cliff, which Scott had already played so effectively in *Dawson's Creek*. So J.J. Abrams and Matt Reeves decided to go with the egg they already had in the basket. In early 1998, Scott got the call he had been waiting for. He'd been cast in the pilot episode of *Felicity*. He would be playing Ben.

"Scott is someone guys want to be and girls want to date," J.J. Abrams says of the reason he wanted Scott to be part of his new show.

While Scott was thrilled to be cast as a regular character in a show that had potential for being picked up by the WB, he couldn't help but feel a slight bit of disappointment. Deep in his heart, he felt a closer connection to the role of Noel than he did to Ben.

"Noel was a character I hadn't played before," he says. "I'd always played the jock. I had a desire to play a character with a little more depth."

Noel was also the character that Scott felt was more like his true self, especially when it came to women. "Around women, we both get extremely nervous. He has a habit of not necessarily stuttering but putting his foot in his mouth, and I seem to do that, too."

Scott says that most of his relationships with women, like Noel's, have started out as friendships, and then moved on to something more. "There's that strange line you cross once you stop being friends and start dating. And I still get the jitters until everything works itself out," he told *TV Guide* in the summer of 1999.

Although Scott felt more like Noel, he knew he had been chosen to play Ben. And so he began analyzing the character as best he could, trying to find out what made him tick. As the production date grew nearer, Scott was becoming more and more thrilled to be part of *Felicity*. He couldn't wait for taping to begin.

Scott's excitement was dampened, however, by a call he received just days before production was to begin on the pilot show. The producers asked him to come in for a meeting at their offices.

"They sit me down and I'm thinking, 'Oh, man, I'm getting fired,'" he recalled in *Entertainment Weekly*. "But then they say, 'We can't find anyone to play Noel. We know you can play both [roles]. Would you play him?' And at that point I'm just happy I still have a job. I'm like, 'Yes, of course! Anything! Can I empty your garbage?'"

So in the end, everything worked out beautifully—just the way Scott had hoped. He had the role of Noel, and Scott Speedman, a young actor from Canada, took on Ben's brooding character.

Too bad things don't always work out that well for Noel and Felicity on the show.

Fame, Fortune, and the Excitement of Success

Even before *Felicity*'s fall 1998 premiere, the show started getting a lot of positive buzz. The press had seen clips from the pilot and met the stars, and they liked what they saw. Without a doubt, *Felicity* was the most highly anticipated show of the 1998–1999 season. So even before the first show aired on September 29, 1998, Scott's life had been changed forever.

Suddenly, Scott was getting recognized wherever he went. "It's weird," Scott admits about his newfound fame. "I was never really recognized until *Felicity* went on the air. But [fame] is exactly what I expected, and nothing like I expected . . . It's ego-building and, at the same time, I can see how people feel trapped by it." His popularity grew so quickly that his guest turn on an episode of the WB's sitcom *Zoe, Duncan, Jack & Jane* in early 1999 was hyped as a major event.

Luckily, Scott has been able to avoid the traps of fame by sticking close to the people who understand what he is going through on a daily basis—his *Felicity* costars. Scott says that the stars of the show, Keri Russell (Felicity), Scott Speedman, Amy Jo Johnson (Julie), and Tangi Miller (Elena), hang out together often—in what little free time they have.

"When we're not shooting, Scott Speedman and I shoot a lot of hoops," he says. "My game's not too bad. I played some in high school, but it's gone downhill a little since. But I really hang out with everybody."

Lately, he's also reportedly spending time hanging around with his girlfriend of nearly a year, Jennifer Garner. Although Scott doesn't like to talk about their relationship, preferring to keep things private, the two have been seen out and about at Hollywood functions.

Scott is truly living the young actor's dream. He's on a hit show, he's making good money, his handsome face is plastered all over magazines, and he has fans all over the world. He even had a high-profile role in the hit movie *Scream 3*, alongside Neve Cambell and Courteney Cox.

But it isn't the fame and fortune that are keeping Scott happy these days—it's the work.

"The best part is that [this job] is a dream come true," he says. "I've always wanted to be a working actor, and the good part is . . . well, it's all good!" he exclaims. "I work long hours, but it's amazing. They pay me. That's amazing. And I get to kiss Keri Russell, and that ain't too bad."

And how does Scott feel about being considered a sex symbol?

"It doesn't make sense," he told *TV Guide* in the article in which he was named one of TV's sexiest stars. "My dad will see this, and laugh his head off."

Scott's dad may laugh, but to the actor's millions of fans, Scott Foley is no laughing matter.

Fast Facts

Full Name: Scott Foley
Birthday: July 15, 1972
Astrological sign: Cancer
Favorite sport: Basketball
Favorite films: *Forrest Gump, St. Elmo's Fire*
Favorite activities: Traveling, tennis, running, sailing, reading
Favorite actor: Marlon Brando
Favorite singer: Kenny Loggins
Tattoo: A small picture of Saint Christopher on his shoulder

Joseph Gordon-Levitt
An Alien in Hollywood

Once upon a time, TV aliens were men from Mars with antennae that rose from the tops of their heads. Not any more. These days, aliens are total hotties! Consider Tommy Solomon, an adult alien intelligence officer who has taken the form of a human teenager—with the sexy brown eyes and thick dark hair of Joseph Gordon-Levitt.

"I've never gotten to play anything besides a kid before, and now I'm playing not only an alien but also a man and a kid," he told *Tiger Beat* magazine of his role on the hit TV series *3rd Rock from the Sun*. "It's so different from anything else. This is the kind of role you hope to play."

And if the character of Tommy is somewhat,

well, *different* from other teenagers on earth,
that's something Joseph can totally relate to.
Unlike other teen celebs, Joey (as his friends
call him) doesn't pal around with the stars. He
actually chooses to be around kids his age who
don't care about what he does for a living.
Rather than attending big Hollywood parties,
he spends his time surfing the Web for chats
about comic-book collecting. He rarely allows
himself to be photographed, and he doesn't
enjoy being interviewed, either.

"I try to stay out of [the teen magazines]
with all my effort and all my might," he explains. "There's nothing on this planet that I
hate more than the teen magazines. Unfortunately, lots of people read them, so I publicize
my work in them. Any time they ask questions
about me, I answer about the movie [he is pro-
moting]."

If the truth be told, Joey loves acting, but
there isn't much he likes about being famous.

"The whole concept of celebrity pisses me
off," he says. "It's such a weird concept that society has cooked up for us. Astronauts and
teachers are much more amazing than actors . . . We have cameras following Monica
Lewinsky, yet teachers in my school have a really hard job, and they don't get any of the
recognition they deserve."

A star who thinks teachers are more important than actors who bring in big box-office dollars? Say things like that in Hollywood, and people will look at you as though you are an alien!

Getting Started

Even before he was performing professionally, Joey knew his home was on the stage. In fact, he was discovered by a Hollywood agent while he was singing with an amateur children's choir in southern California. It was 1987, and Joey was just six years old, but he already had that star quality that makes you the center of attention no matter how many other people are around you.

Joseph's first job was eating peanut butter in a TV commercial that ran on the West Coast. He was only six and a half years old at the time, but he knew from that moment on that acting was what he was meant to do. And he was good at it, too. A week after landing the peanut butter gig, Joey found himself on the set of the TV film *Stranger on My Land*, which starred veteran actor Tommy Lee Jones. Joey played the character Rounder.

At the time, Joey had no actual acting training; he was going on instinct. But that doesn't mean that he thinks everyone can do that—or that casting producers should just pick kids off the street to play roles in films or on TV.

"Sometimes it can yield excellent actors," he says of the practice of hiring nonactors for roles. "But sometimes, it's stupid. Often, casting directors think anyone under twenty can't act, so they find a kid who they think *is* the character. But it all depends on the situation. I'm a perfect example. I play an alien and started that when I was fourteen. I assure you, however, I am a terrestrial."

After his work on *Stranger on My Land*, Joey went on to do other made-for-TV movies, including *Danielle Steel's Changes* and *Hi Honey— I'm Dead*. He also had a regular role on the 1991 series *Dark Shadows*.

Dark Shadows was actually a remake of the mid-1960s show of the same name. It was an afternoon soap opera with a supernatural twist—the main character, Barnabas Collins, was a vampire! The show went off the air after just a few years, but it was shown in reruns for decades, and developed a big cult following. In 1991, it was brought back as a prime-time series with a new cast.

Joey was cast as series regular David Collins, a nephew of Barnabas. Unfortunately, the series didn't last very long. Neither did Joey's next series, *The Powers That Be*, which was a political comedy created by producer Norman Lear.

So for a while Joey made a career of taking on guest-starring roles on prime-time hits like

Family Ties, *thirtysomething*, and *Murder, She Wrote*. He had a recurring role on *Roseanne* as George, D.J.'s hilariously boring best friend.

In 1992, Joey hit the big screen for the first time, with a small role in *A River Runs Through It*. In the film he played the young version of the character Norman, who was played later in the picture by Craig Sheffer.

A River Runs Through It made a star of Brad Pitt, but it didn't have quite the same magic for Joey. In fact, he would continue working in small roles on TV and in the movies for two more years until stardom would be within his grasp.

Angels in the Outfield: A Home Run!

In 1994, Joey was offered the leading role in the Disney live-action film *Angels in the Outfield*. The movie was about a young boy who believed he saw real angels helping the California Angels baseball team win games.

The character of Roger was a difficult and complex role for Joey. Naturally, the character is cute and funny—just as Joey is in real life. But the character had a sad side to him as well. In the film, he is placed in temporary foster care by his father, who sarcastically remarks that they will be a family again when the California Angels win the pennant. Naturally, Roger starts praying for a miracle—which is what it looks like it'll take for the Angels to actually win. But in the movies, miracles do happen, and with the help of a few heavenly angels the baseball team starts winning.

Angels in the Outfield featured a stellar cast of pros—Danny Glover played the manager, and Tony Danza took on the role of an aging pitcher on the team. But it was Joey who got the notices, eventually winning *The Hollywood Reporter*'s Young Star Award for his part in the film.

Suddenly, Hollywood sat up and took notice. Joey's next film role was no kiddie film. He played Demi Moore's son in the psychological thriller *The Juror* in 1996. In the film, Demi's character tries to protect her son, Oliver (who was played by Joey), from a group of mobsters.

The Juror was big box at the office. Now, Joey was on the A-list of Hollywood kids.

Landing on the 3rd Rock from the Sun

In 1996, Marcy Carsey and Tom Werner were hatching an idea for a unique show about aliens who land on earth. The aliens' mission is to observe human life forms. To do that, the aliens must take on human form and live together as an earthbound family. They called the show *3rd Rock from the Sun*.

Marcy and Tom had managed to score a big-name cast, including Oscar winner John Lithgow as the family's leader, Dick, and comedienne Jane Curtin as his human love interest. They'd cast newcomers French Stewart and Kristen Johnston as aliens Harry and Sally Solomon as well. But the pair were in a bit of trouble when it came to casting their oldest alien, who would have to live in the youngest body; a character named Tommy Solomon. They just couldn't find a teen who could play an old alien in a young, hormonally charged teenage body.

Then Marcy and Tom remembered a kid who'd had a recurring role on one of their other successful series, *Roseanne*. He was the one who played George. They'd always thought he was talented. After careful consideration, Joey was offered the role of Tommy.

Now, some people might say that taking on a role in a TV series just as his movie career was taking off was not a great move. But Joey has a view that is unique among actors in Hollywood. As far as he is concerned, a good part is a good part.

"They are completely different," he says of roles for movies and TV. "It's different audiences. I like a live audience [like the one *3rd Rock from the Sun* tapes in front of], but I enjoy them both. You can't make a comparison about which is preferable. It's like comparing apples and oranges."

In this case, Joey chose to accept the part of Tommy on *3rd Rock from the Sun.* Not surprisingly, his portrayal of the offbeat character made him the apple of Hollywood's eye. To date, the cast of *3rd Rock from the Sun* has won two Screen Actors Guild Awards for outstanding performance by an ensemble. Joey himself also scored his second *Hollywood Reporter* Young Star Award for his individual work on the show.

Being part of an ensemble cast on a successful series made it possible for Joey to continue his movie career as well. Because his work on *3rd Rock from the Sun* made him so visible, offers from movie studios began pouring in fast and furiously.

Joey chose a large role in *Sweet Jane,* an independent film that got shown at a few film festivals, as his first film project after joining the cast of *3rd Rock.* But don't feel left out of the party if you've never heard of *Sweet Jane.* The film has never been released in theaters.

"It's one of the main things I'm proud of," Joey says about his work in *Sweet Jane.* "There's no distributor for it now, though."

If *Sweet Jane* was a small film, destined for obscurity, Joey's next film got a whole lot of hype—if only because it marked the return of scream queen Jamie Lee Curtis to the horror-film genre. *Halloween H20* was a frightening flick released in 1998, twenty years after the original *Halloween* movie hit the big screen. (Get it? *H20* is *Halloween*, twenty years later.)

The original *Halloween* was a surprise hit—a small-budget movie that went on to earn millions at the box office and to spawn several sequels. It also launched Jamie Lee Curtis's career. But *Halloween H20* was a huge project from the start, with a cast that included Curtis, Adam Arkin, Michelle Williams, and LL Cool J. Joey was thrilled to be part of the *H20* cast—although he was only given a small part, a neighborhood kid who winds up being a victim of a mass murderer.

"When I did [*Halloween H20*], I only signed on for the first five minutes . . . They told me: 'Work for a few days, get money, and get an ice skate in your face,'" he jokingly told a chat room audience.

In the film, Jamie Lee Curtis once again plays Laurie Strode, the woman who, twenty years before, had been terrorized by Michael Myers. When *H20* begins, she's moved to another town and changed her name, hoping Michael Myers won't find her—or her seventeen-year-old son, John (played by Josh Hartnett).

Of course, Michael Myers does find her, and

he begins to terrorize her and everyone in her new neighborhood, including Jimmy, the character played by Joey.

To no one's great surprise, *Halloween H20* was a huge hit—partially because it rode the wave of teen horror flick success that had started with *Scream* and *I Know What You Did Last Summer*. Nineteen-ninety-eight was the year that teen films began to take over the box office. Joey was definitely in the right place at the right time!

A Shakespearean Success Story!

Scripts were pouring in to Joey's house in late 1998. It seemed like everyone wanted the young star of *3rd Rock* to have a part in their next film. But none of the scripts seemed to interest Joey—until he read a modern-day version of William Shakespeare's play *The Taming of the Shrew*. It was called *10 Things I Hate About You*.

"The teen film trend is kind of sad in a way," he told a chat audience shortly after making *10 Things*. "You get one good movie like *Scream*, and then you get a bunch of business executives who say, 'That made money,' so they try and replicate it, making mediocre crap. It's sad, because they think teens can't tell the difference. Before *10 Things*, I read a lot of lousy scripts and thought I wouldn't do a movie. Then I found *10 Things*. It's based on Shakespeare, and that's awesome."

10 Things certainly was different. And the teens who saw it understood just what Joey was talking about. They went back to see the film again and again, making it one of the highest-grossing teen movies of 1999. Fans especially loved Joey's portrayal of Cameron, the shy new kid in town who instantly falls in love with Bianca, the most beautiful girl in school. Unfortunately, Bianca isn't allowed to date—until her older sister, Kat, does. And Kat is one nasty girl. It's up to Cameron to find a guy who is willing to date Kat.

Coming Back Down to Earth

Today, Joey can honestly say that he has been a member of the casts of several successful films and a hit TV show—at the same time. That's not a claim many actors can make. But Joey has no desire to rest on his laurels. Right now, he's not only taping new episodes of *3rd Rock* and looking at film scripts, he's developing his musical chops as well. Joey plays guitar and drums, and does a little singing—that's really him performing in the garage band on *3rd Rock*. He's into blues, rock, funk, and jazz. One day, he'd like to record his music.

As if that weren't enough, he's looking at colleges. Joey knows that nothing—not even a huge acting career—can replace an education. After college, he hopes to direct movies.

No matter what his future holds, Joey will surely remain one down-to-earth guy (which is a bit odd for an alien, doncha think?) who doesn't take celebrity seriously, and only values his art.

What should you do if you happen to run into Joey at a restaurant, a comic-book convention, or Rollerblading by the ocean (the places he's most likely to be spotted)? Well, here's a helpful hint, right from the horse's mouth.

"Just walk up and say, 'I like your work,'" he tells his fans. "But if you don't like it—don't say anything."

Judging by how wonderful Joey's work is, his fans are sure to have plenty to talk to him about!

Fast Facts

Full name: Joseph Gordon-Levitt
Nickname: Joey
Birthday: February 17, 1981
Astrological sign: Aquarius
Parents: Jane and Dennis
Favorite book: *The Catcher in the Rye*
Favorite movies: *The Big Lebowski* and anything else by the Coen brothers
Hobbies: Gymnastics, comic books, flag football, Rollerblading

Seth Green
The Ultimate in Cool

You'd be surprised just how much actor Seth Green and his *Buffy the Vampire Slayer* character, Oz, actually have in common. For starters, neither one has had what you would call a *normal* high school experience.

In Seth's case, he was kind of an outsider at school—and not because a few days out of the month he grew a really heavy beard and howled at the moon. (That's Oz's werewolf domain.) Seth's problems in high school stemmed from the fact that he was absent a lot because he was working. Even during his childhood, Seth had a healthy film career, appearing in movies with big-name stars, like *The Hotel New Hampshire* with Jodie Foster, Woody Allen's *Radio Days*, and *Big Business* with Bette Midler. By the time he reached the age of nine, he'd already appeared on *Saturday Night Live*. But while playing all those different characters may have fulfilled Seth creatively, it didn't help his social life one bit. In fact, Seth's career kept the other kids away, much in the same way garlic chases off vampires.

"To work in your chosen career from the time you're seven and be allowed to leave school to work on movies sets you apart from people. I wouldn't say [the other kids] were jealous or resentful, it's just that they don't know how to handle it because it's a weird thing," he explains.

The peer rejection was hard to take. In fact, Seth says that his lack of popularity was more disappointing than any "don't call us, we'll call you" he ever got from a casting agent.

"True rejection is when you are standing on a kickball field and people are picking teams, and you are the last one picked, begrudgingly," he recently told *TV Guide*. "Because then, you are being judged more personally than [you would be by] any casting director."

In Seth's real-life high school, he was pretty much alone in the "different" department. (Not too many child stars come out of Philadelphia—it's not like in New York or Los Angeles, where every other kid seems to have a bit part in a movie or to be starring in a commercial.)

At *Buffy*'s Sunnydale High, however, there's a whole crew of kids who are different—whether they be vampires, vampire slayers, or werewolves like Oz.

For Seth, it's nice to finally fit in.

"It's a pretty tight group," he says of his *Buffy* costars. "I love Alyson [Hannigan, who plays Willow]; we're old friends . . . I like Nick [Brendon, who plays Xander] a lot and Charisma [Carpenter, who plays Cordelia], and when Sarah [Michelle Gellar, who plays Buffy] is around, it's great!" he remarks.

Just as he did during his real-life school career, Seth spends his time off the Sunnydale High set doing extracurricular work and acting in big-money movies, like the two *Austin Powers* laugh fests, the teen flick *Can't Hardly Wait*, and Will Smith's action-thriller *Enemy of the State*. The only difference is that now he's got friends who understand his need to act. Mostly, that's because his new friends are actors, too. In fact, Seth's two closest buds are Ryan Phillippe (*Cruel Intentions*) and Breckin Meyer (*54*).

"The three of us have been talking about producing stuff," Seth says of these acting Three Musketeers. "We're very serious now. We're all in good positions. But we're being really selective. We don't want to make something stupid or meaningless. We want to make something great, or at least make a great attempt."

And his fans are waiting with bated breath!

Growin' Up in Front of the Cameras

Seth Green was born in Philadelphia on February 8, 1974. His family could not have been more normal. His dad was a math teacher. His mom was an artist. He had an older sister with whom he got along, usually. So how did this guy turn into the Seth Green we know today—the one who dyes his naturally red hair blue, yellow, black, and magenta whenever the mood strikes him, and who gets his kicks from playing a werewolf in front of thousands of TV viewers?

Well, it all started when Seth was around six. He suddenly got this notion that he wanted to be an actor. His parents were not in total agreement with his plans. "But I just pushed and pushed," Seth recalled during an on-line chat. "Sometimes you just know what you want to do."

For most kids in Seth's hometown, that would have been the end of it. Philadelphia is not exactly the land of agents and managers. But in Seth's case, his uncle just happened to be a casting director. He arranged for Seth to find a manager. The manager sent Seth and his mom on a two-hour drive into New York City to go on auditions.

Seth's cute little face and flaming red hair were a commercial casting agent's dream. Before long, it was hard to turn on a show without seeing Seth's face smiling back at you during the breaks. There he was, hawking everything from Kodak film to Burger King fries.

By the time he was eight, Seth found himself in the big time—he'd scored a part in the movie *The Hotel New Hampshire*, which also starred brat-packer Rob Lowe and multi–Oscar winner Jodie Foster. Seth recalls the older actors being "really great" to work with. Especially Jodie, who had been a child actor herself.

The roles kept coming. In 1986, he had a small part as Malcolm in the film *Willy Milly*. A year later he played Chuckie, the annoying kid brother in the teen comedy *Can't Buy Me Love*.

The year Seth turned twelve, he received a phone call that most actors wait their whole lives for. Famed director Woody Allen was on the line. He wanted Seth to star in his movie *Radio Days*.

Starring in a Woody Allen movie almost guarantees that an actor will be thrust into the limelight. And that's exactly what happened to Seth. Unfortunately, at the tender age of twelve, Seth was not exactly ready for life as the man of the hour. He readily admits that he became totally obnoxious regarding his fame. (His official bio actually says he became "cocky," but "obnoxious" may be more like it.) Perhaps the ugliest moment came when Seth went on *The Tonight Show* and tried to joke around with the king of late-night TV, Johnny Carson. Seth thought he was being funny, but the results were disastrous.

"You get wrapped up in the money and people telling you how great you are," Seth says of his younger days. "You forget you are pretending."

Although he continued acting, it would be a long time before Seth would see that kind of fame again. After *Radio Days*, he was cast in a few more movies, including *My Stepmother Is an Alien* (which, coincidentally, also featured his future *Buffy* costar Alyson Hannigan), *Big Business*, and *The Day My Parents Ran Away*. He got regular roles in a few TV series, like the short-lived *The Byrds of Paradise* and the aptly titled *Temporarily Yours* (the show didn't even last a full season), and had a small part as young Richie in Stephen King's TV miniseries, *It*. Plenty of one-shot roles followed on regular series, but his characters were incidental parts, with single names like Bob, Wayne, and the Emcee.

None of those films or TV shows brought Seth the kind of recognition he'd seen in his late-1980 *Radio Days* days. To make things worse, as he got older, being a cute little red-head stopped counting for much with casting directors, who were looking for more conventional types for their teen-oriented films. There were quite a few roles Seth went for and didn't get. Ironically, Seth says, that is exactly what saved him from himself.

"The failures keep you humble and sane. They make you realize how fleeting any form of success is," he explained to *TV Guide*.

The Tide Begins to Turn

When Seth finished high school, his parents wanted him to go on to college. "It was alluded to that my . . . adult acting career might not be successful," Seth admits of his parents' desires. "But to me, a fallback plan suggested that I might fail. And I have never, ever wanted to invite that into my world."

Luckily, Seth's parents' worst nightmares were never fulfilled. By the late 1990s, Seth's career started to pick up—thanks to funny man Mike Myers.

For years, Mike Myers had been secretly creating a bizarre character—a retro British James Bond type who had neither the brains, looks, nor crime-fighting prowess of the real 007. He just thought he did. Mike called the character

Austin Powers. And in 1997, Mike decided to bring Austin to life on the big screen.

In the film, Mike played two characters—Austin and his nemesis, Dr. Evil. When Mike decided that Dr. Evil needed a smart-mouthed son to drive him crazy, he went knocking on Seth's door.

Austin Powers: International Man of Mystery was the surprise hit of 1997. The relatively low-budget film turned a huge profit, and entered the public's consciousness in a way nothing had for a long time. Suddenly, everybody everywhere was walking around repeating Austin's signature sayings, like, "Groovy, baby." Working on *Austin Powers* was a fun, if not particularly easy, job. According to Seth, the toughest part was keeping a straight face while working with Mike Myers. In one scene, it became so impossible for Seth to keep from cracking up that, after shooting take after take, the director just decided to leave the laughter in.

"You do see me laugh in the scene where Mike is coming at me with his arms out-stretched, saying, 'Don't look at me like I'm Frankenstein.' I'm clearly smiling," Seth points out.

Soon after the release of *Austin Powers*, Seth was about to have even more to smile about—being cast as a regular on the series *Buffy the Vampire Slayer.*

Life's a Howl!

When Seth Green was originally cast as Oz, a teenage werewolf who meets up with Buffy, he expected to be on the set for a only few weeks. He was originally contracted to appear in just four episodes.

But from the minute Oz appeared at Sunnydale High, the fans were mesmerized. Like the character of Willow, who developed a big crush on Oz, fans immediately latched onto Seth's quirky portrayal of a guy who, according to the show's creator, Joss Whedon, "would have the same reaction to spray cheese as to true love." Before he knew what was happening, Seth's contract was extended—first to five episodes, and then to eight. By the show's second season, Seth had signed on as a regular supporting cast member—meaning he would appear in all twenty-six episodes in the 1998–1999 season.

It's a little-known fact, but playing Oz was not Seth's first acquaintance with Buffy and her vampire enemies. In 1992, he had filmed a few scenes for the *Buffy the Vampire Slayer* movie, which had starred Kristy Swanson as Buffy and featured *Beverly Hills 90210*'s Luke Perry. But don't go renting the flick searching for Seth. You won't find him. As so often happens in Hollywood, Seth's scenes were left on the cutting-room floor. (He was to suffer the same fate years later, when his scenes as the voice of a cat in Eddie Murphy's *Dr. Dolittle* were also cut from the film.)

One of the things Seth likes most about the *Buffy the Vampire Slayer* series is that the look of the show is so slick. In fact, according to Seth, "Doing *Buffy* is like doing a film, except the schedule is tighter."

Seth says that the cast and crew of *Buffy the Vampire Slayer* "take their monsters pretty seriously." That means that having the creatures of the night look as realistic as possible is a top priority. And while that may thrill the fans, imagine what it does to Seth—who has to turn into a fur-covered werewolf.

"[Makeup] takes a lot of time. It's very difficult to stand still. It starts at 11:30 A.M. [and continues until] 4:30 P.M. They have to hand-lay all the hair on me, but the makeup artists there are so great—sweet and considerate. They make it as painless as possible. The end result is worth the effort."

Movie Mania

As we all know, Seth's not a werewolf, he just plays one on TV. On the movie screen, he sticks to more human characters (although some might call those characters subhuman!). In 1998's *Can't Hardly Wait*, Scott played Kenny

Fisher, a rap-dude wannabe who tries to be too cool for his school, but is really just looking for love. Seth says it wasn't hard to get into the character's brain, or to develop his walk and speech patterns. As he told *USA Today*, "I listened to a lot of *Yo! MTV Raps*. Watch anything with Puffy Combs and you're on it!"

Seth followed up *Can't Hardly Wait* with a role in the high-profile Will Smith thriller *Enemy of the State*. He played Selby, a member of a government team that is pursuing Will Smith. It was a very small part—you might not even notice Seth unless you were looking for him—but it was one he just had to take.

"It's not my movie. It's Will Smith and Gene Hackman's," he told E! Online. "I have a really small part, but the reason I wanted to do it is because Tony Scott is one of the best action directors in the world."

In 1999, Seth continued his work on *Buffy the Vampire Slayer* while also taking on three other TV roles. But don't go channel-surfing looking for Seth's sexy smile on-screen. In these three series, only his voice is recognizable. He plays Nelson Nash on the animated series *Batman Beyond* and Chris Griffin, part of the cartoon clan on *Family Guy*. He also provides the voice for the kid bully-turned-dog in Nickelodeon's *100 Deeds for Eddie McDowd*.

The last year of the millennium also saw Seth

taking on some high-profile movie roles. First out of the gate was *Stonebrook,* a film-festival favorite that had Seth taking the lead role for a change. He played Cornelius, a con man who gets his roommate, played by Brad Rowe, and his friends involved in a con ring. When the guys get caught, the police force them to help catch a big-time con artist.

Next up was the sequel to *Austin Powers: International Man of Mystery,* 1999's *Austin Powers: The Spy Who Shagged Me.* Seth reprised his role as Scott Evil for the flick. He had so much fun with the part that he has reportedly signed on to voice the character in the highly anticipated animated *Austin Powers* TV series.

He also had a supporting role as Mick in the controversial 1999 film *Idle Hands. Idle Hands* is the story of a teenager (played by Devon Sawa) who wakes up one morning to discover that one of his hands is possessed by the devil—and bent on committing murder. The film tanked at the box office, but *Idle Hands'*s failure had nothing to do with quality and everything to do with timing.

In the spring of 1999, two teenagers went on a killing spree in their real-life high school in Littleton, Colorado. The country was devastated by the senseless killings that occurred inside the school. *Idle Hands* was released that summer, perhaps too soon after the Littleton murders. Americans just weren't in the mood for a film about teen terror.

Idle Hands wasn't the only Seth Green project affected by the killings in Littleton. The 1999 season finale of *Buffy the Vampire Slayer* was delayed by several months because it, too, involved violence at a high school.

Although Seth says that he's "just an actor," and that he can't solve the world's problems, he did feel the need to voice an opinion on the U.S. government's insistence that Hollywood shares the blame for the rash of in-school teen murders that plagued the late 1990s.

"When tragedies like Columbine happen, everybody wants a face . . . to blame it on. Movies, TV, and video games are easy targets," he told *TV Guide* in the summer of 1999. "Well, if you want a target, let's look at the gun lobbies that have so much power in Washington that they keep the Congress, the president, and the people from really addressing the situation."

The *Buffy* episode eventually aired in July of 1999, to some of the strongest numbers the show had ever seen.

Coming Up

So what does the future hold for Seth Green? Well, we hope, many more seasons of *Buffy*, for starters. Though he's taking a leave of absence from the show to concentrate on movies, Seth's not about to pull a star trip and bite the vampire-slaying hand that feeds him. He and the producers have left the door open for him to return to the role of Oz in the future. And though Seth is hoping to make a real name for himself in movies, he's getting very particular about the ones he does make. That's why Seth is so serious about eventually producing his own movies.

For now, though, he's happy to have supporting roles in films that catch his rather, er, *unusual* fancy. His next movie, due out on Halloween of 2000, is called *Attic Expeditions*. Seth plays a recovering psychotic in a mental institution.

One thing Seth would like a little more of in the future is enough time for a relationship to blossom. At the moment, he's totally single, despite instant Internet rumors that he and Alyson Hannigan have a real-life romance that echoes their on-screen chemistry. Seth insists they are just friends, and that they hang out together because they've known each other for so long— since the old *My Stepmother Is an Alien* days.

Of course, it might not be easy for Seth to find just the right woman. After all, who wants to get involved with a guy who turns into a werewolf weekly, and has a father who is as "evil" as his last name?

Well, according to the fan magazines, where Seth has become a regular, there are thousands of girls out there ready to take on the role of Seth Green's gal! And Seth was number one in E!'s list of hot young Hollywood stars in 1999.

So for all those kids who picked Seth last for the team in high school—eat your hearts out, baby!

Fast Facts

Full name: Seth Gesshel Green
Birthday: February 8, 1974
Astrological sign: Aquarius
Parents: Herb and Barbara
Sister: Kaela
Hobbies: Playing pool, going to the movies
Favorite movies: *Midnight Run* and *Raising Arizona*
Favorite actors: Kevin Spacey, Shirley MacLaine, Kevin Bacon

Joshua Jackson
King of the Creek

It may be impossible to believe now, but the first role Joshua Jackson auditioned for on *Dawson's Creek* was the role of Dawson himself. Hard to picture, huh? Josh doesn't display any of the deep, brooding seriousness of Dawson, does he?

That's what the producers thought as well. So they offered Josh a chance at the show's sidekick position—Pacey Witter. They felt that the wisecracking, girl-getting Pacey was more up Josh's alley. And you know what? They were right.

"There's not a whole lot of acting required," Josh admits about playing Pacey. "I'm generally a fairly boisterous, occasionally obnoxious guy."

Sound like any TV character you know?

Okay, so Josh really likes the character of Pacey. But the show is called *Dawson's Creek*. How does he feel about someone else having the lead role he once coveted?

"Number one second banana is a most worthy mantle to wear," he declares proudly.

Besides, while Pacey may be the second banana on the show, Josh is the *Dawson's Creek* cast member who is number one in the fans' hearts. Just check the pages in the teen mags or the fan sites on the Web. Hey! Maybe they should change the name of the show to *Pacey's Place*.

Just Joshin'

Joshua Jackson was born on June 11, 1978. Although he entered the world in Vancouver, British Columbia, he spent the first few years of his life in San Francisco, California. It was in San Fran that Josh first discovered his love of entertaining when he joined the city's famed San Francisco Boy's Chorus. (Betcha didn't know Josh could sing as well as act!)

When Josh was eight years old, his family moved back to Vancouver because his mother got a high-powered job as the casting director for a weekly hour-long ABC drama called *Mac-*

Gyver. Like many shows today, *MacGyver* was being shot in Canada.

Thanks to his mom's job, Josh got an early look at the goings-on on a TV set, and he liked what he saw. By the time he was nine, Josh was begging his mom to send him to her casting agent friends for auditions.

But Josh's mom and dad were not too hip on the idea of having an actor for a son. His mom had worked with a lot of professional children, and she was concerned that Josh would be spending far too much time in an adult world and not enough time being a kid. Still, Josh wouldn't let up on his mom, and, eventually, she gave in.

Josh went on a flurry of auditions, and finally landed his first role when he was ten years old. He appeared dressed in a cowboy uniform on a commercial pushing Canadian tourism. (How cute does that sound?) The ad was the first glimpse Americans had of Josh, since the ad ran only in the States.

After proving that he could handle the professional demands of acting, his mother arranged for Josh to have a guest-starring role on an episode of *MacGyver*.

Although his on-screen jobs then dried up for a while, Josh never stopped acting. He took parts in Canadian regional theater. At one point, he had the lead role of Charlie in a stage version of *Willy Wonka and the Chocolate Factory*. Once again, Josh got to sing in public. This time he had a solo, performing the song "I've Got a Golden Ticket."

It was while he was working in theater that Josh learned a helpful trick to get him through every actor's worst nightmare—forgetting his lines.

"If I can't remember a line, I start asking a lot of questions until it comes to me," he reveals. "So whenever you hear me say, 'You understand?' or 'You know what I mean?' that means I am completely lost and just buying some time."

Theater helped Josh develop his acting chops in many ways, and, by 1991, he was ready for the big time. He was cast in the film *Crooked Hearts*.

Crooked Hearts featured a cast of up-and-coming stars like Juliette Lewis, Jennifer Jason Leigh, and Vincent D'Onofrio. Although Josh had one of the smallest roles, just being part of the ensemble was a great educational experience.

"I learned so much about acting and movies by being on the set," he recalls of his *Crooked Hearts* experience.

Once Josh was part of the movie circle, he was quickly cast in another film. And this one was everything it was "quacked" up to be.

Makin' the Most of *The Mighty Ducks*

In 1992, Walt Disney Pictures was busy casting their newest film, *The Mighty Ducks*. Emilio Estevez had already been cast as the unwilling coach of a less-than-stellar kids' hockey team. The producers were looking for just the right kids to take on parts as the not-so-skilled hockey players.

Because he is Canadian by birth, Josh has always had a fascination with ice hockey—which is not to say that he was a great skater. Still, he figured he had enough skill on the ice to at least get a small role in the film. But he did better than that. Josh scored the role of Charlie Conway, the most reasonable member of the team and Emilio Estevez's on-screen prodigy.

Although some critics dismissed *The Mighty Ducks* as little more than a hockey version of *The Bad News Bears* (a film about a Little League baseball team made up of misfits and coached by an unwilling Walter Matthau), the film really struck a chord with moviegoers. In fact, to this day, Josh still gets asked about the movie and the two *Mighty Ducks* sequels that followed.

"This girl came up to me and said, 'You're Charlie from *The Mighty Ducks*,'" he told *Twist* magazine in June of 1999. "It was sweet and flattering, but then she proceeded to get the other three busloads of kids and I spent the next hour answering questions about *The Mighty Ducks.*"

Sorry, Josh, there's no ducking your *Duck* days! He even made reference to them on *Dawson's Creek*, when his character, Pacey, identifies Emilio Estevez as the guy "in those *Ducks* movies! Man, those were the best."

The Mighty Ducks finally got Josh the notice he deserved. New roles followed fast and furious. For the next four years, Josh found himself on movie sets, with parts in not only the *Mighty Ducks* sequels but in films like *Digger, Andre, Magic in the Water,* and *Tombstone.* He starred in Showtime movie specials, too, including *Robin of Locksley,* an updated version of Robin Hood also featuring Devon Sawa, and *Ronnie and Julie,* a modern-day Romeo and Juliet story between a figure skater and an ice hockey player. (Hmmm . . . do we sense a pattern here?)

But while Josh's professional life was finally taking shape, his home life was a disaster. Soon after the successful release of *The Mighty Ducks,* Josh's parents split up. He felt as though his world was crashing down around him.

"It was painful because everything you trusted and felt secure about fell apart," he remembers of his feelings at the time.

Josh tried to let out his frustrations by play-

ing sports. To some extent, bouncing basket-
balls and whacking baseballs helped. But Josh's
distress over his parents' split began to show itself in more destructive ways. Josh had always
been a self-described "class clown" in school,
but now he was a downright troublemaker. He
was disruptive in class—when he actually got
there. According to Josh, he was kicked out of
school twice. "Once for attitude and once for
lack of attendance. I'd like to say that that was
because I was working a lot, but the truth is, I
was a real pain."

Although Josh went on to get a General
Equivalency Diploma, he says that today one of
his biggest regrets is not actually finishing high
school. And while he is not currently in college,
he plans on going one day. In the meantime, he
reads everything he can get his hands on, trying
to self-educate. "Any knowledge is good knowledge," he says. "So the more you read, the better."

Eventually, Josh came to grips with his parents' divorce, and was able to straighten out
his life. In 1996, he auditioned for a teen horror film called *Scream 2*. Josh was not cast as
one of the major leads in the 1997 blockbuster
(his character was so incidental he had no
name—the credits read only Film Class Guy
#1), but the movie was about to change his
life.

Welcome to *Dawson's Creek*

Scream 2 was written by Kevin Williamson, who is highly regarded as one of the best screenwriters in the industry when it comes to teen-driven projects. While he was busy working with the cast of *Scream 2*, Kevin was also looking for teens to cast in his new television project, which was being produced for the WB network. The show, as if you didn't know by now, was to be called *Dawson's Creek*.

Josh heard about the casting call for *Dawson's Creek* while he was on the set of *Scream 2*. He hightailed it off the movie set and went to read for the role of Dawson.

Although he didn't get the leading role, Josh was thrilled to be cast as Pacey. In fact, when the cast all met on the Wilmington, North Carolina, soundstage where the show tapes, Josh was the happiest camper of them all, by all reports. He truly loved the character, and was anxious to bring him to life.

"Pacey is a flawed character," he explains. "You get to see the imperfections, the chinks in his armor. Dawson's righteous and intensely self-analytical. Pacey's a guy who can't help but live for the moment."

The cast of *Dawson's Creek* was pretty much isolated in North Carolina; at the beginning of production, the only people they knew were each other. That made them close, like a real family.

"When *Dawson's* started, the four of us [cast members Joshua, Katie Holmes (Joey), James Van Der Beek (Dawson), and Michelle Williams (Jennifer)] hung like eighteen hours a day because we didn't know anybody. We were a mini-family. Now we know things about one another that we shouldn't."

In fact, Joshua and costar Katie Holmes got so close that for a while they were an "item" on the set. The two have since broken things off, although they remain friends. Josh is totally single at the moment.

When *Dawson's Creek* went on the air, Josh got caught up in all the excitement that comes from being on a TV show that has positive "buzz" in the industry. He got to walk down the red carpet at his first big premiere (for the film *Godzilla*), and was flown, along with the rest of the cast, to a press junket in New Orleans. Josh was more than a little excited about what his future held.

Josh got a whole lot of attention during the early days of *Dawson's Creek*, and not only for his acting. In 1998, during the show's first season, Josh had what can only be classified as the "juiciest" story line on the show. Pacey was having an affair with his red-hot English teacher!

So how did Josh feel about his kissing scenes with a sexy older woman (actress Leann Hunley)?

"It was quite nice, thank you. I had to do a lot of takes on that," he joked to Globenet. "I was impressed with how graceful she was with it. She was having pangs of guilt because of the teacher-student coupling."

The story line brought a huge response—and a lot of publicity—to the fledgling show. For the most part, kids thought Josh did a great job as Pacey. But certain folks, particularly adults, were upset by the plot. Some even went so far as to complain about Josh being chosen for one of those famous "got milk?" mustache ads.

The ad shows Josh with a glass of milk. It reads "Women of all ages look up to me. Why? I'm six foot two. Thanks in part to milk."

Funny, right? Well, the Dairy Education Board, a group that believes dairy products are not necessarily healthy, didn't think so. They complained that the dairy industry was "endorsing the crime of statutory rape."

But Josh was totally nonplussed about the controversy. He was just glad people were talking about *Dawson's Creek*—and about his portrayal of Pacey.

Pass the Popcorn, Please!

Now that Josh is a big-time teen idol, movie producers are knocking on his door. In 1998, fresh from shooting the first season of *Dawson's*

Creek, Josh took on the role of Damon Brooks in the fright flick *Urban Legend*. Josh dyed his hair blond to play one of a group of teens who begin to die or disappear in ways that mimic different legends or horror stories that have been told over the years.

A year later, Josh was again part of a controversial teen media circus when he joined the cast of the teen sexual drama *Cruel Intentions*, which starred Sarah Michelle Gellar, Ryan Phillippe, and Reese Witherspoon. Once more, Josh was in the position of being a supporting actor, but he made the most of it, playing Blaine Tuttle, a gay student who is dared to bring his lover out of the closet.

Josh's next on-screen appearance was a lot less contentious. But, then, there's rarely any controversy surrounding a Muppet movie. In 1999's *Muppets from Space*, Josh had a cameo role—as Pacey from *Dawson's Creek*. He was only on-screen for less than a minute, but that was enough to bring thousands of teen girls into the theaters—something unheard of in the Muppets world.

Josh followed up screen time with Gonzo and Kermit with two movies about college life. The first was *Gossip*, a film about a crowd of college kids who are given an assignment to spread a rumor and then observe what happens. In the second movie, *Skulls*, Josh played a college student who is invited to join a secret society at Yale University and becomes involved in a murder mystery.

But just because he has become a full-fledged movie star, don't expect Josh to be leaving *Dawson's Creek* in the near future. "I hope the show runs forever!" he says sincerely.

So do his millions of fans. After all, movies only come around once. *Dawson's Creek* is a weekly event!

Fast Facts

Full name: Joshua Carter Jackson
Nickname: Josh
Birthday: June 11, 1978
Astrological sign: Gemini
Mother: Fiona
Siblings: Sister Aisleagh and stepbrothers Lymon and Jonathan
Distinguishing mark: A red birthmark next to his belly button
Pets: A turtle named Searesha, a cat named Magic, and a dog named Shumba
Favorite movie: *Good Will Hunting*
Favorite TV show: *The X-Files*
Favorite books: *The Lord of the Rings* by J. R. R. Tolkien
Heroics: Josh saved four female swimmers who were stranded off the coast of Wilmington, North Carolina, during the summer of 1999. He and a friend jumped in to save the swimmers and kept them afloat until the Coast Guard came and brought everyone to safety.

Chris Klein
He Gets Everyone's Vote

Sometimes you just have to be in the right place at the right time. Ask actor Chris Klein. He was walking out of his high school gym when he literally bumped into film director Alexander Payne. Alex was scouting locations for his soon-to-be-filmed picture, *Election*.

"He was with my principal, getting the nickel tour [of Millard West High School]," Chris recalls, "and we got introduced. I was real excited that a director was at my high school. But I didn't think much of it, and we went our separate ways. Later, I found out that my principal had told him how I'd always been interested in acting and that I was in school plays and all that," he says.

The principal must have done some selling

job on Chris's acting chops, because soon after, Alex called Chris and asked him to audition for the role of a dim-witted jock named Paul Metzler in *Election*.

"I thought, 'What the heck,'" Chris recalls. "I might as well go for it."

Smart move. *Election*, which starred Matthew Broderick as Paul's teacher, went on to be one of the most critically acclaimed films of the spring of 1999. And Chris in particular got great reviews.

But that didn't come as a surprise to Chris's high school buddies. After all, Chris was a former high school jock playing a high school jock. It was the "dumb" part of the dumb jock character that took a lot of acting on Chris's part.

The Making of a Star

Chris Klein was born on March 14, 1979, in Chicago, Illinois. From a very early age, he knew his heart was in acting.

"I dreamed about acting ever since I was a kid," he recently told E! Online. In fact, he had his first acting experience when he was in the fourth grade. He was part of a community theater production at the Sheraton Convention Center in Chicago. His performance of the song "This Little Light of Mine" was so adorable that the applause nearly ripped the roof off the place. From that moment on, Chris was hooked.

"I thought, 'Wow! Glitter!' After that, whenever I saw a video camera, I wanted to be in front of it."

But before Chris could become a local celebrity in Chicago, Chris's dad was transferred to Omaha, Nebraska. It was not a change Chris was particularly happy about. And to make matters worse, he totally embarrassed himself on his very first day in his new junior high.

"I remember it like it was yesterday," he recalls. "It was the second day of seventh grade and I didn't know what to expect. I was nervous. I walked into the commissary and threw up in front of everybody."

Well, you can say this for the guy—he sure knows how to make an entrance!

But Chris's reputation for having a bad stomach didn't last. Before long, he was caught up in school sports, making a name for himself on the swim team and as the linebacker on the Millard West High School football team.

"I thought high school was the pinnacle for me," he says. "My high school experience was really fun. I wore a letter jacket, dated a cheerleader—that sort of thing. I drove around in a Camaro Z28."

Having the cheerleaders shout his name at the games was a rush for Chris, but it didn't totally fulfill his need to be applauded for his performing talents. Luckily, his high school also happened to have a performing arts program. Chris got involved with the theater group, and eventually snagged the lead role of Tony in his senior class production of *West Side Story*. And his performing didn't stop there.

"Whenever there was a project at school that called for a video camera, I recruited all my friends," he recalls.

By the time Chris graduated from high school, his classmates had long gotten past that notorious junior high lunchtime fiasco on Chris's first day of school. In fact, they honored him by naming Chris Mr. Millard West, signifying just how many pals he had made. Taking part in both the sports and theater programs had helped Chris make a ton of friends in school. But he never dreamed it would help him create a whole new career.

Vote for Chris

Not long after that fateful meeting with Alexander Payne, Chris auditioned for the role of Paul Metzler, the dumb jock who runs for student-body president in *Election*. And from that very first screen test, it was obvious that Alexander

Payne's first impression had been correct. Chris was a natural in front of the cameras. Alexander offered Chris the role. Naturally, Chris jumped at the chance to star in his first film.

But, as is often the case in Hollywood, production on the film was postponed. Chris took advantage of the delay in production to begin taking classes at Texas Christian University. But he only lasted four weeks at college. He had to leave the books and frat parties behind when he finally got the call to report to work.

"The movie got postponed, and [Alexander Payne] didn't use my high school, but he cast me anyway," Chris explains.

Even though he had never gone to acting school, Chris was able to do what all good professional actors must do—study the script and come up with the motivation for his character's actions.

"The thing about Paul is, he doesn't get it. He's the high school quarterback in a Midwestern town. And you know what that means. But Paul doesn't. Paul doesn't realize the influence that he can have on the student body. He doesn't get that he can have any girl he wants. He doesn't understand, and not only that, he's shy with people," Chris explains.

Election was a critical hit—if not exactly overwhelming at the box office. Film reviewers loved the black comedy aspects of the film, and felt that star Matthew Broderick (who played Chris's faculty adviser during his campaign for student-body president) had given one of the best performances of his career. Praise was high for Chris and Reese Witherspoon (who played Tracy, the oh-so-ambitious high-schooler who runs a tough campaign against Paul), as well. One reviewer called Chris "angelic," while another said that he could "make a whole career out of playing sensitive but not-too-bright hunks."

And for a while it seemed as though that's just what he was going to do. As *Election* was opening in theaters (to a lukewarm reception from moviegoers, who weren't sure whether the comedy was aimed at teens or adults), Chris was busy putting the finishing touches on his next movie—the raunchy teen comedy *American Pie*. Once again, he played a dumb jock. This time the character's name was Oz. But instead of trying to get a position in the student council, this movie character was going for something a lot more basic—the girl of his dreams.

In *American Pie*, lacrosse team star Oz joins the choir to get closer to a shy girl named Heather for whom he has fallen—hard. Since Chris had been on his high school football team *and* had sung in school musicals, the role was a natural.

Chris was especially psyched about being able to sing. "It was really fun," he told *TNT Rough Cut* of his duet with costar Mena Suvari, who plays Heather. "We recorded the song and it turned out fantastic. The people that mixed it did a fantastic job. And then we did the scene, and all we had to do was lip-synch. We had a good time with it, just started hamming it up."

Chris says he believes *American Pie* will eventually become a classic teen film that will live on and on, like the 1980s teen flick *Fast Times at Ridgemont High*. "Everybody still sees *Fast Times* as soon as they are old enough to pop it in the VCR," Chris says of the film that launched Sean Penn's career. "Shoot, if *American Pie* can be that for the 1990s, how lucky am I to be a part of it?"

A Tasty Performance

American Pie was quite possibly the most controversial film of the summer of 1999. That was no small feat, considering that it was the summer that brought Stanley Kubrick's steamy *Eyes Wide Shut* to the screen. *American Pie* was a teen comedy that took a look at the one thing all teens seem to have in common—a fascination with the opposite sex. Although the movie's target audience was teenagers, it wound up earning an R rating, which meant that anyone under age seventeen would not be admitted to the theater without an adult. Still, teens managed to find a way to see the film, making it one of the highest-grossing films of the summer of 1999.

Chris says the film's popularity is really easy to understand. "Being cool or sophisticated is not what [American Pie] is about. It really is all about laughing—at ourselves, mostly. I don't know for sure, but I bet most people can relate."

Even though the film made big bucks, the R rating infuriated Chris and his costars. They didn't understand why the film was given the restricted rating. The movie was tame, compared to other films that had been given the same R rating.

"The same people were praising There's Something about Mary last year for being refreshingly outrageous, and that movie went much further than we ever do," Chris said, defending the film. "American Pie is not more offensive than Porky's or Fast Times at Ridgemont High were in their day."

The film's producer, Chris Weitz, spoke for the cast and crew when he explained to the Toronto Sun, "We wanted to make a movie for kids that showed real high school kids. Not that '80s world of John Hughes [a director of teen-oriented films] that just doesn't exist."

Although Chris Klein was part of an ensemble cast in *American Pie*, it was his name that seemed to get the biggest headlines after the movie's release. *Variety* praised his performance, describing Chris as "hunkier and even better looking than Keanu Reeves. The guy's got 'movie star' written all over him."

In typical Chris Klein modesty, he told *New York Now* that it wasn't necessarily his acting that made the character of Oz so popular. Chris felt a lot of the credit had to go to the writers. "There's no other role I would have played," he said. "What you have to bring to art is yourself, and [when I read the script] I felt Oz in myself. He spoke to my heart."

Moving On

Although Chris says that he would someday like to get his college degree, he knows that now is not the time. His movie career keeps him too busy to hit the books. In fact, it's keeping him too busy to even get an apartment.

"I'm pretty homeless," he told E! Online. "I live out of a suitcase. I sleep on airplanes. I don't have a permanent place in Los Angeles, but I spend a lot of time there."

During the latter part of 1999, Chris made his home in Minneapolis, Minnesota, while filming *Here on Earth*, his third movie.

"I play a rich prep-school kid with this corporate macho-man father who spends a summer in a small town," he explains.

His role on *Here on Earth* will be a big departure for Chris. This time, there's nothing funny about his character, or that of his costar Leelee Sobieski. She plays Chris's love interest, a girl with a terminal disease.

Here on Earth will give Chris a chance to show that he can do more than play the "dumb jock" part. And he is confident that his fans will accept him in a different persona.

As for his personal life, Chris—unlike Oz, who finally realizes what it means to really love someone—is completely single, and not necessarily by choice.

"I think I'm a hard guy to date right now. I'm never around. Dating's not a priority for me. I'm really enjoying work."

Maybe so, Chris, but remember that adage about all work and no play. There are plenty of girls out there who would love to have a date with a talented, gorgeous guy who is as American as . . . well . . . apple pie!

Fast Facts

Full Name: Christopher Klein
Birthday: March 14, 1979
Astrological sign: Pisces
Parents: Fred and Terri
Siblings: Sister Debbie and brother Tim
Height: 6'1"
Favorite actors: Jimmy Stewart and Tom Cruise
Favorite snack: His mother's homemade cookies
Favorite sports: Swimming and football
Workout routine: Pumping iron, two hours a day, every other day

Ashton Kutcher
That '70s Hunk

Where do you think most actors get discovered—New York? Los Angeles? London? Paris? How about Homestead, Iowa—population 100?

It may sound hard to believe, but that's where Ashton Kutcher was living when a talent agent spotted him and suggested he enter a statewide modeling contest. (Which, being the gorgeous hunk he is, he won!)

"I was like, 'Do guys do that?'" Ashton recalls. "I thought Fabio was the only male model. And I didn't fit that bill."

Maybe not. But Ashton did fit the bill of modeling agencies who were looking for a fresh, all-American face to launch fashion lines by designers like Calvin Klein, Gucci, and Gianni Versace. Before he knew it, Ashton was traveling the world, walking down runways in New York, Paris, and Milan. And he was making a lot more money than he ever had when he had a job vacuuming cereal dust around the Cheerios line at the Iowa General Mills plant.

Fresh off the Farm

Still, it wasn't necessarily Ashton's sizzling good looks that got him the role of Michael Kelso on Fox's *That '70s Show*. It was his energy, his enthusiasm, and his ability to understand what it's like to be a teenager growing up in a really small Midwestern town.

"[When you are a small-town teenager] you're sincerely believing you are living in the most boring town on the face of the earth," Ashton explains. "You have to find your own fun. I kind of grew up doing that, so I'm able to relate to the character in the show."

Can he ever. The town Ashton grew up in was really, really small. In fact, there were only one hundred people living there. "There was nothing to do," Ashton says of his teenage years in Homestead. "It was a keg in a cornfield and cow-tipping."

Not that a lack of action and excitement was bad. In fact, after the turmoil of his younger life, being a teenager in a quiet town was just fine for Ashton.

Ashton's early years were actually spent in Cedar Rapids, Iowa. His father worked for General Mills. His mother stayed at home and cared for Ashton, his fraternal twin brother, Michael, and his older sister, Tausha. Life was fun for the family—until 1991, the year Ashton and Michael turned thirteen.

Suddenly, Ashton's world was turned upside down. His parents separated and began divorce proceedings. Then Michael came down with a disease called myocarditis, which is a viral inflammation of the heart. Michael needed a heart transplant, and Ashton stayed by his side the whole time.

"He showed me the love one brother has for another," the now-healthy Michael recalled in a *People* magazine article.

Once Michael's safety was ensured, Ashton's mother packed up her three children and moved them to Homestead. There, Ashton discovered his two great loves—sports and acting. He joined the football team and took part in school theater productions. His first role was the thief in his seventh-grade production of *The Princess and the Crying Goose*.

"I broke the boundaries," he remembers proudly. "It wasn't cool to be in plays—especially if you were in sports. And I was in both."

Ashton had a lot of friends in high school (his brother, Michael, recalls that Ashton "always got all the girls"), but deep in his heart he knew the small-town life was not where he wanted to be. "I wanted to come to Hollywood," he told *People* magazine. "But in Iowa, it's like, 'However do I do that?'"

And while Ashton was looking for a way to come to California and act, he enrolled at the University of Iowa and began majoring in biochemical engineering. (Hey, just because you play a really dumb guy on TV doesn't mean you don't have brains, right?) He planned on specializing in genetics until that talent agent plucked him out of the cornfields and threw him into the limelight.

Going Back in Time

After Ashton's modeling career took off, he branched into commercials, scoring a Pizza Hut ad before he had the confidence to try his dream and fly out to Hollywood. In 1997, he joined the throngs of struggling Hollywood actors looking for that one big break by going out on audition after audition. The thing that set Ashton apart from the other actors was the fact that he was offered two of the first parts he auditioned for—one for a role on NBC's *Wind on Water*, and another on *That '70s Show*. Ashton went for the comedy. Considering that *Wind on Water* didn't even make it through one season, it would appear that Ashton made the right choice.

Once Ashton was cast as Kelso, he began trying to find ways to relate to a character who has been described as "most handsome, but probably can't spell the word 'handsome.'" Obviously, he couldn't relate to Kelso on the intelligence level, but he could bring some understanding of what motivates Kelso and his friends to act the way they do.

"Kids in the 1970s didn't have computers and CD players," he explains. "They had to come up with different ways to have fun. And that's what the show is about: finding different ways to have fun."

Although everyone on the set recalls Ashton being a complete pro his first day on the set, Ashton says *he* will always remember that day as a disaster.

"I was petrified," he told *All-Stars* magazine. "I was really scared when we did the first read-through. The first time you see a script, you do a read-through at a table. Everybody was sitting there, and I didn't really know what was going on. I was shaking. I had a pencil and I snapped it."

But when it came to portraying Michael Kelso on camera, Ashton came through with flying colors. And although the main character on the show is actually Eric, played by Topher

Grace, Ashton almost immediately became the boy most likely to see his face on the cover of a teen magazine. In fact, Ashton's dark-haired good looks, along with his ability to play a not-too-bright hunk with great sensitivity, have caused people to compare him with a true teen dream from the real 1970s, John Travolta!

It may be hard to believe now, especially since he is highly regarded as an actor drawn to intelligent, dramatic characters, but twenty-five years ago, John Travolta came to America's attention by playing one of TV's hottest—and stupidest—characters, Vinnie Barbarino on *Welcome Back, Kotter.* John parlayed that success into some major films, like *Saturday Night Fever* and *Grease.* Those movies propelled John Travolta to icon status. Critics think Ashton has the same potential.

But being voted the most handsome member of the *That '70s Show* cast is not necessarily something Ashton is completely comfortable with. In fact, he says that being considered good-looking can cause problems for an actor.

"Casting agents think you can't play psychos," he laments. "I guess they think that most criminals are ugly. I disagree with that. I definitely don't want to be stuck in the pretty-boy category."

Made for the Movies

While casting directors may not be considering Ashton for those psycho roles, they are placing him in some pretty high-profile places these days. When he's not wearing puka-shell necklaces and bell-bottoms on the set of *That '70s Show*, he's in front of movie cameras, making feature films with some of Hollywood's hottest stars. And while he's still not the leading man, everyone admits it is hard to watch anyone else when Ashton is on the screen. Of course, as everyone knows, sidekicks often steal the show.

Ashton started with a film called *Reindeer Games*, a thriller that stars Ben Affleck and Gary Sinise. He will be following that one with *Coming Soon*, a sexual coming-of-age film set in Manhattan and featuring actors Yasmine Bleeth, Mia Farrow, Spalding Gray, and Gaby Hoffmann. In *Down to You*, another film set in the Big Apple, he shares screen time with Freddie Prinze, Jr., Julia Stiles, and Selma Blair; and in *Texas Rangers*, he joins a group of kids who band together to clean up the West after the Civil War. Ashton's fellow hot Hollywood stars James Van Der Beek and Rachael Leigh Cook play other members of the *Texas Rangers* gang.

But if all this big-screen excitement has you concerned that Ashton will lose his down-home sweetness, relax. You can take the boy out of

Iowa, but you can't take Iowa out of the boy. In fact, Ashton has no patience for those Hollywood types who use their relationships for publicity and do charity work only if it will get written up in the papers. Ashton has also publicly refused to name the woman he is currently dating, preferring to "stay mysterious about it," even though the publicity from a relationship would be enormous. And although he spends some time each week doing charity work, you won't be seeing photographers following him around while he helps others. "I don't want people to think I visit hospitals and talk to kids for a photo op," he explains. "To me, that's using a charity to make a name as a good guy. I have always felt that it's important to give back."

And here's a word of caution. If you ever become a star out in Hollywood, don't waste your time complaining about anything to Ashton.

"These Hollywood people who are making umpteen thousand dollars a week and they're not happy with it, well, I'm like, 'How can you not be happy?' I was never able to buy a new car. I washed dishes in a kitchen in Homestead. I worked in a butcher shop skinning deer . . . jobs like that. Sometimes, I can't believe how ungrateful people can be."

"Ungrateful" is not a word folks in Hollywood can use to describe Ashton, that's for sure. He is fully aware of the fact that he is very lucky to be a bona fide overnight success.

"I feel bad in a way because so many people struggle for so long out here before it happens," he told *Us* magazine. "But I don't believe that old cliché that good things come to those who wait. I think good things come to those who want something so bad they can't sit still."

Nancy Krulik

Fast Facts

Full Name: Christopher Ashton Kutcher
Birthday: February 7, 1978
Astrological sign: Aquarius
Parents' names: Father: Larry Kutcher; mother: Dianne Portwood; stepfather: Mark Portwood
Siblings: Older sister Tausha and twin brother Michael
Favorite book: *Where the Red Fern Grows* by Wilson Rawls
Favorite actor: Al Pacino
Favorite musicians: Beck, Janis Joplin, Creedence Clearwater Revival
Favorite TV show: *Jeopardy*
Hobbies: Golf, snowmobiling, and playing Nintendo

Matthew Lawrence
Oh, Brother!

Matthew Lawrence was born in a small town just outside of Philadelphia, the City of Brotherly Love. And that's a perfect fit, because Matthew is part of a family of acting brothers—his big bro, Joey, and his younger sib, Andrew, have both graced the airwaves as well. Coincidence? Maybe. But the truth is, no one is better at portraying family feelings on TV than Matthew Lawrence.

For many years, Matt almost made an entire career of playing his older brother, Joey, in flashback sequences of shows Joey starred on, like *Gimme a Break!* and *Blossom*. Later, Matt, Joey, and Andy played brothers on their own sitcom, *Brotherly Love*. Matt played the middle brother on that one. (Talk about typecasting!)

Today, Matt's on his own, as part of the cast of ABC's long-running TGIF staple, *Boy Meets World*. But some things never change. Once again, Matt is playing a brother. Only this time, he's Jack Newman, the older half-brother of Shawn Hunter.

Matt: Heather Locklear's Honey!

Acting was a part of Matt's life from the day he was born, on February 11, 1980. By that time, his brother Joey was already heavy into the business, having won a "cutest child" contest at Strawbridge & Clothier (a Philadelphia department store) when he was only five and having moved quickly into commercials. So Matt can't remember a time when words like "auditions," "callbacks," "scripts," and "rehearsals" weren't part of the family vocabulary.

All his life, Matt has worshiped Joey. In fact, it was only recently that he told a chat audience, "My older brother, Joe, is probably—no, definitely—my biggest hero." It was only natural that Matt would want to follow in his big brother's footsteps and throw his hat in the acting ring as well.

Like Joey, Matt saw a lot of early success in his career. His very first role was on a highly rated prime-time soap opera called *Dynasty*. The show told the story of a wildly

wealthy family. The cast included such lumi-
naries as Joan Collins and John Forsythe. It
also featured a sexy blond newcomer named
Heather Locklear, with whom Matt had the
most scenes. He played her three-year-old son,
Danny.

"It was a long time ago," Matt says of his
early scene-stealing work with *Melrose Place*
and *Spin City*'s hottest vixen. "I really don't remember much."

Maybe not, but at the time casting directors
sure found Matt memorable. Not only did he
find work on the *Dynasty* set, he also spent time
making all kinds of commercials, including one
of the famous Jell-O pudding spots that featured Bill Cosby.

For a while, Matt shuttled between Los
Angeles, where *Dynasty* was taped, and Abing-
ton, Pennsylvania. But eventually the moving
around proved to be too much. He and his family moved to Los Angeles, so that Joey and Matt
could continue their careers.

Matt was only on *Dynasty* for one year before
he landed a featured role on the sitcom *Sara*,
which starred future Oscar winner Geena
Davis. He played Davis's young son, and although the show didn't last long, it did give
Matt far more screen time than he had ever had
on *Dynasty*. And that only meant good things
for his career.

Challenges

On *Dynasty* and *Sara*, Matt didn't have to do much acting. He just sort of had to be cute on camera. Which was not hard—considering that even back then he had a smile that would melt your heart. But in 1988, when Matt was only in second grade, he took on a role that even veteran actors might find challenging. He played the title character in the made-for-TV movie *David*.

David told the true story of David Rothenberg, a boy who was caught up in a terrible custody battle between his parents. Matt says playing David was the toughest role he's ever had.

"I was young, maybe eight or nine, and I had to play this boy David, who was burned over ninety-five percent of his body," he recalled on a Disney chat line. "It was a horrible but true story."

Matt was very convincing in his portrayal of David. Suddenly, newspapers and magazines that had been referring to him as Joey's little brother, or, even worse, "Lawrence Cutie #2," began to see Matthew as a talent in his own right. Offers rolled in, and Matthew took on roles in feature films like *Planes, Trains & Automobiles* and *Tales from the Darkside: The Movie*, as well as TV projects featuring major Hollywood players, like John Ritter in *The Summer My Father Grew Up* and Melissa Gilbert in *Joshua's Heart*. He also had the chance to act opposite two entertainment-biz legends when he played the grandson of Brian Keith and Cloris Leachman in *Walter & Emily*.

David wasn't the only tough role Matt took on in 1988. He also made the switch from baby of the family to middle brother when the littlest Lawrence brother, Andrew, was born.

"Some people say that being the middle brother is hard," Matt acknowledges, "but I think I'm really lucky. I get to have an older brother *and* a younger brother."

No Doubt About It, Matt's a Star!

Many people might say that Matthew, Joey, and Andrew (who is also now in the acting business) missed a great deal of their childhoods by spending so many days on the sets of TV shows and movies. But Matt would be the first to argue that being an actor actually *enhanced* his younger years.

"My parents did a great job of making sure we had a really balanced situation," he says. "I think acting is really fun. I love doing it, so I don't really think I missed that much."

Besides, if being a kid means spending as much of your time as you can having fun, Matt had a real advantage over other children. After all, what could be more fun than spending months hanging around on a movie set with wacky actor Robin Williams? That's just the opportunity Matt had in 1993, when he was cast in the role of Chris Hillard in the comedy *Mrs. Doubtfire*. Once again, Chris played a kid caught in the middle of a bitter custody battle. But this was no heavy drama. *Mrs. Doubtfire* was primarily a comedy, with Robin Williams playing Matt's dad. In the film, Robin's character is banned from being with his kids, so he decides to rejoin his family incognito—by dressing up as a woman and becoming a nanny to his own kids.

Matt loved being part of the *Mrs. Doubtfire* family. After all, with Robin Williams around, you never knew what was going to happen next. But Matt says that besides being a great guy, Robin is also a phenomenal actor who was always willing to help out his younger costars.

"It was a great experience working with an actor like that," he says of Williams. "The whole thing was like one of those dreams coming true."

Mrs. Doubtfire was one of the biggest hits of 1993. And although much of the critical kudos went to Robin Williams, it was Matt who captured the hearts of the girls who went to see the film over and over and over again.

No doubt about it—*Mrs. Doubtfire* had turned Matthew Lawrence into a full-fledged teen dream. Suddenly, his face was plastered all over the covers of fan magazines. He was a hot property where the kids' market was concerned—and the powers that be in Hollywood were quick to find him another place where he could strut his stuff.

In 1994, Matt took on the leading role in the syndicated sci-fi TV series *Superhuman Samurai Syber-Squad*. The show, which jumped on the mid-1990s teen-as-superhero bandwagon started by the *Mighty Morphin Power Rangers*, developed a following both with little kids and with older girls. While the small ones were fascinated by the bash-boom fighting scenes, the teen fans were more interested in the show's leading man. They flooded Matt's costar Jayme Betcher with queries about what Matt was like as a kisser (Jayme played Matt's girlfriend on the show), but the actress refused to kiss and tell. Instead, she told a *Teen Beat* editor at the time that Matt was "talented, confident, and *absolutely* adorable!"

No secret there!

Brotherly Love

Superhuman Samurai Syber-Squad lasted only one season, which meant that by 1995, Matt was looking for work. Coincidentally, Joey's show, *Blossom*, had reached the end of its long run, and he was looking for jobs as well. Andrew, the littlest Lawrence, was seven years old, and itching to follow in his big brothers' professional footsteps.

The solution to all of their problems came in the form of *Brotherly Love*—an NBC sitcom that starred the Lawrence boys as (what else?) brothers!

Brotherly Love first aired in September of 1995. Matt says that he has never had so much fun on a set. "We just love it when we work together," he says. "When we got to play brothers in . . . *Brotherly Love*, we definitely had chemistry together, because we're brothers in real life. That was my favorite role."

Part of the fun of *Brotherly Love* was the writers' desire to bring some of the real-life Lawrence brothers' experiences on to the show.

"A lot of the scripts came from things that happened in our own lives," Matt recently confided to a chat audience, "but, like any show, there's things they needed to put into the show format."

Of course, there were some uncharted dangers on *Brotherly Love*. Matt remembers that one of his most embarrassing professional moments occurred on the garage set of the show.

"We have a lot of motorcycles on the set because Joey's character works in a garage. I was walking to my dressing room, and I wasn't really doing anything, so I sat on this motorcycle," he told a *16* magazine editor in 1996. "I guess the kickstand wasn't all the way in, and it flipped over. Those things are like five hundred pounds. The whole audience saw it. I wasn't hurt, just embarrassed."

That's okay, Matt. You're so cute when you blush!

Despite the fact that Joey, Matt, and Andy were having a great time working together on *Brotherly Love*, the show never was a hit with the NBC viewers. The network canceled the show after just one season.

But that wasn't the end of the show. Joey, Matt, and Andy were determined to keep working together, so they arranged for *Brotherly Love* to be moved to the fledgling WB network. The show continued there for one more season, until finally being canceled in 1997.

Brotherly Love wasn't the only family project that the Lawrence brothers put together during the mid-1990s. They also shared the screen in a made-for-TV movie called *Brothers of the Frontier*.

Boy Meets *Boy Meets World*

Even though Matthew loves working with his brothers more than anyone else in the world, by

1997 it was clear that in order to keep his career going ahead full steam, he would have to go back to being the only Lawrence brother in the cast. His first step in reigniting his solo career was to join the cast of the already well-established ABC sitcom, *Boy Meets World*.

Matt took on the role of Jack Newman, Shawn's older half-brother in the series' fifth season. If coming into a series so late in its run was difficult, Matt never showed any signs of the strain. Matt says that's because the cast members welcomed him and went out of their way to be helpful and friendly. Danielle Fishel, who plays Topanga on *Boy Meets World*, even went so far as to agree to go to Matt's senior prom as his date in 1998. But don't jump to any conclusions—Matt and Danielle (who once dated Lance Bass from the pop group 'N Sync) are just buddies.

"We're good friends, and I was very single when my prom came, so she was nice enough to escort me there," Matt insists, being every bit the gentleman.

At first, Matt and his character, Jack, had very little in common. Although both are really "good guys," as Matt puts it, Jack lacked some of Matt's sense of fun. But as he has continued playing the role, Matt says he and Jack have more and more in common.

"When you play or create a character, you always add a little bit of yourself in at the time," he explains.

Still, there is something Jack has done that Matt says is a definite "no" in his book. Jack started a romance with his female roommate, which threw a wrench into his friendship with his friend Eric (played by Will Friedle).

"If I had a best friend, I wouldn't let a girl come between us," Matt vows.

Ironically, Matt's best friend these days (other than his brothers, of course) would probably be Will Friedle. Besides playing most of their *Boy Meets World* scenes together, Matt and Will also joined forces to make a 1999 made-for-TV movie called *H-E Double Hockey Sticks*. In the film, which also stars veteran comedienne Rhea Perlman as the devil, Will plays a devil in training who tries to sabotage the career of Matt's too-cool hockey dude character.

What Does the Future Hold?

These days, Matt's one of the busiest guys in L.A. Besides having a regular supporting role on one of ABC's highest-rated sitcoms, he's also a college student. Although he hasn't chosen his major yet, he's dropped hints that he might get a degree in business, or that he might follow his childhood dream of becoming a zoologist. Matt just loves animals!

You might wonder why such a successful actor would even bother getting a college degree. "A lot of actors think that they don't need college because they already have a career," he admits, "but that's a bad idea. Hollywood is fickle; your career can end pretty fast. If the acting jobs dry up, you have to have something to fall back on. In fact, my advice to kids interested in acting is to make sure you get an education, too."

As if college and *Boy Meets World* weren't enough, Matt is also taking on movie projects. He can be seen in the film *The Hairy Bird* (originally titled *Strike*), which stars Kirsten Dunst and Gaby Hoffmann as classmates in an all-girls school. The ladies are in an all-out war to stop the school from merging with a nearby boys' prep school that Matt's character, Dennis, attends.

Matt also recently got a chance to team up with his brothers again to make the film *Family Tree*. The movie stars Andy as a young boy who fights his entire town to save an old oak tree from being torn down. Matt took on the role of Andy's older brother. And, not to be left out, big brother Joey wrote a few songs for the *Family Tree* soundtrack.

With so many great projects already under his belt, you might think Matt would feel secure in his status as a terrific young actor. But the truth is, he sees himself as "a work in progress. I think that if I keep working my entire life, I might have something that I am proud of."

Matt's most important goal, he says, has nothing at all to do with his career. This family man would someday like to have a family all his own.

"I really want to meet that perfect girl and be a dad someday," he says, adding quickly, "but not for a long time, though."

Hmm. *Boy Meets Girl*. It's got a nice ring to it.

Fast Facts

Full Name: Matthew William Lawrence (When Joey was born, the family's last name was Mignona, but they legally changed their name to Lawrence soon after Joey was born. Both Matt and Andy were born with the last name Lawrence.)

Birthday: February 11, 1980

Astrological sign: Aquarius

Parents: Joseph and Donna

Siblings: Joey and Andy

Favorite foods: His grandmother's eggplant Parmesan and Sour Patch Kids

Favorite animal: Cats

Favorite band: The Dave Matthews Band

Favorite sports: Basketball and baseball

Favorite things to do with friends: Go to dinner and a movie or go bowling

Matthew Lillard
The Screen's Sexiest Psycho

According to Matthew Lillard, there are a lot of real psychos in the world. "There must be a wee bit of psycho in everyone out there," he insists. "I think that everyone has those dreams, those delusions, those ideas of, 'Oh, I'd love to kill him. I hate him!' I just get paid to play them out."

Does he ever! In the past few years he's made a career out of playing guys who are nuts—like Stu, the psychotic sidekick to Skeet Ulrich in *Scream*, Stevo, the wacked-out rebel in *S.L.C. Punk!* or *Wing Commander*'s Todd "Maniac" Marshall. In fact, it seems that no matter what the role, Matthew puts his own personal psycho spin on it.

"Psychos are so much more fun to play [than

traditional leading men]," Matt admits. "I just get into them and have a blast. I have the best time. And people seem to accept me as a psycho."

Now, most folks might be insulted by that. But Matt wears it as a badge of honor. After all, it takes a lot of work to become a believable nut case.

"You don't want to come across as an idiot," Matt explains. "You want to come across as a strong psycho, not some cheesy killer. It takes a lot of energy. I'm not the one who gets the girls. I'm usually the one that kills them."

All in a day's work.

In real life, Matt is actually more of a lifesaver than a killer. In fact, he actually once saved the life of a complete stranger.

"I was on a date and this guy had gone into a seizure and swallowed his tongue. I rolled him over and . . . he was clinically dead, I think. He was blue, but I saved him [with artificial respiration]. The next time I went back to that establishment, they gave me twenty percent off."

So there you have it. Matthew Lillard isn't a psycho murderer. He just plays one in the movies. And that's making him one of the most in-demand actors of young Hollywood. But Matthew wasn't always the guy most girls wanted to date. In fact, as a kid, quite the opposite was true.

A Meat-and-Potatoes Kind of Guy

Matthew Lillard was born January 24, 1970, in Lansing, Michigan. In his early years, his family moved around a lot—by the age of seven, he'd lived in four different places. But by the time Matt reached the end of first grade, his family finally settled down in Tustin, California.

While attending the Tustin public schools, Matt wasn't exactly a model student. Instead, he was considered the class clown. Doesn't surprise you, does it? But what you might be shocked to discover is that Matt was not considered even remotely attractive back then. In fact, in high school, the now six foot three, muscular stud was actually short for his age and pudgy. The only way he could get a girl to kiss him was in a game of spin the bottle. We'll bet that a certain Kelly, the girl who gave him that first kiss, is glad today that the bottle landed on her.

Pretty much the only thing that gave Matt joy in high school was being part of the acting crowd. In eighth grade, he took part in a speech class presentation of the play *Greed for Gold*, playing (what else?) the bad guy. And he was brilliant at it!

"I wanted to be an actor because it was the only thing I was ever really good at," Matt recalls. "When you grow up, there's the jock clique, the good-looking clique, and the geeky clique, and I never really fit into any of those. And I was a big kid. I was really heavy until I hit late puberty. My [family is from] the Midwest. In the Midwest, you eat meat and potatoes. You drink a lot of soda pop, and, generally speaking, eat a lot of cheese."

Starting Out

After high school, Matt made an attempt at getting his college degree. But higher education just really wasn't where his heart was.

"I tried a couple of times," Matt says. "I went to college like three or four times and never finished. It wasn't my forte. I knew I didn't want to do biology or math."

So Matt decided to try his hand at professional acting. Soon after high school graduation, Matt slimmed down, toned up, and stretched to become the tall, gorgeous actor type casting directors are searching for. He got his first movie role, as an extended extra in *Ghoulies 3: Ghoulies Go to College*.

An extended extra is an actor placed in several scenes to provide continuity in a movie. The extended extra rarely has any lines, but he is recognizable to the audience. Matthew was lucky enough to actually have been given a line in the film—which was all he needed to earn his coveted Screen Actors Guild (SAG) card.

A year later, Matt made his TV debut on the then-fledgling Nickelodeon kids network. He was chosen to host the network's skateboarding series, *SK8 TV.*

While he was busy being the wacky host of a kids' TV show, Matt continued to work on his serious acting techniques, enrolling in the American Academy of Dramatic Arts in Pasadena, California. When the Nickelodeon show ended in 1990, Matt moved to New York City and attended the prestigious Circle in the Square theater school. He dreamed of having a role in a Broadway show.

Despite auditioning for every role that he read about in *Backstage* (the newspaper New York actors search for word of auditions), Matt never got to see his name in a Broadway *Playbill.* So Matt did something amazing—he moved back to L.A. and started his very own theater company with the help of his pal Dalton Grant. Now, that takes guts!

"When I was twenty-one, I started my own theater company in L.A.," he says. "I was the artistic director of a theater company called the Mean Streets Ensemble. The basic principle was to pay kids fifty bucks a month, and we maintained the theater space twenty-four hours a day. We did twenty-five shows in a year and a half. It was the best thing I ever did."

The Mean Streets Ensemble's first play, *Tracers*, opened on July 4, 1991. The ensemble stuck together for almost a year, until internal politicking caused Matthew to leave. Without his leadership, the Mean Streets Ensemble couldn't stick together.

Besides some great opportunities for acting, the theater company was a great dating service for its performers. There, Matthew got involved in his first serious relationship, with actress Christine Taylor (who later went on to play Marcia in the *Brady Bunch* movies)—although, according to Matthew, she eventually dumped him.

Making It in the Movies

By 1994, Matthew was working pretty steadily in the movie biz. Sure, the parts were small, but at least the work was coming in. In 1994, he appeared in *Serial Mom* and *Vanishing Son IV.* The next year, he followed those films with roles in *Ride for Your Life*, *Animal Room*, and *Mad Love.*

But 1995 was the year that launched Matt

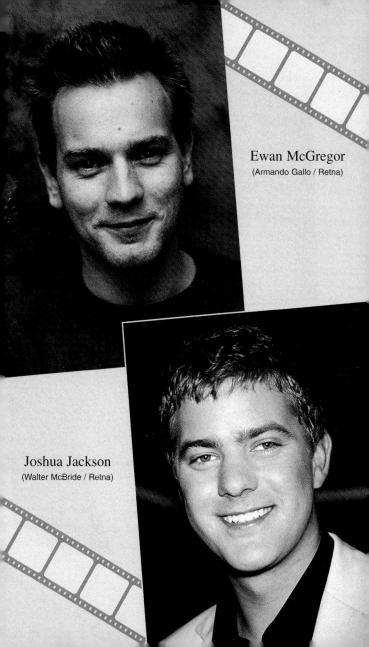

Ewan McGregor
(Armando Gallo / Retna)

Joshua Jackson
(Walter McBride / Retna)

Chris Klein
(Gilbert Flores / Celebrity Photo)

Scott Speedman
(Photofest)

Nicholas Brendon
(NGI / London Features)

Matthew
Lawrence
(Steve Granitz /
Retna)

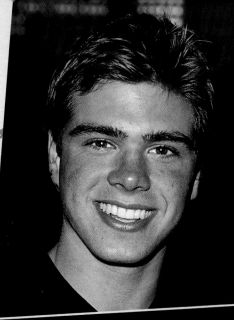

Rider Strong
(Allen Gordon /
London Features)

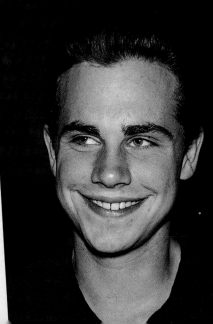

Seth Green
(Gregg DeGuire / London Features)

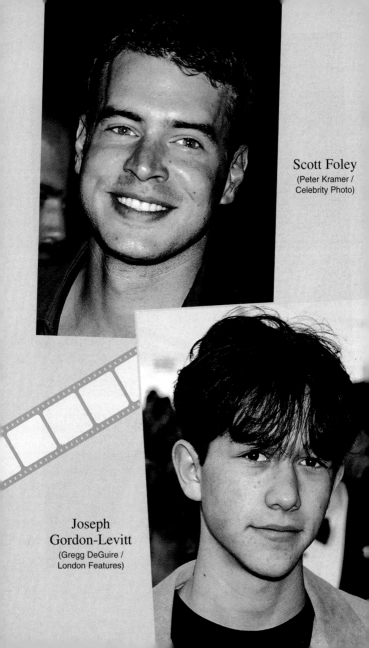

Scott Foley
(Peter Kramer /
Celebrity Photo)

Joseph
Gordon-Levitt
(Gregg DeGuire /
London Features)

Kel Mitchell
(Janet Gough /
Celebrity Photo)

Matthew
Lillard
(Tim Hale /
Retna)

Ashton Kutcher
(Steve Granitz / Retna)

I LOVE MY MOM

Tobey Maguire
(Armando Gallo / Retna)

on his path to psycho stardom. He took on the part of Emmanuel Goldstein (the Cereal Killer) in the cyber-thriller *Hackers*. It was Matt's first on-screen wacko, and he made the most of it.

"My character in *Hackers* was originally written as a stoner," he recalls. "When I talked to the director, we talked about how it could be more interesting if this kid was amped out, kind of elevated. That was a choice. We added the pigtails and the funky clothes. It was a bigger choice than [the way] it was originally written."

Playing *Hackers*'s Cereal Killer got Matt noticed in a big way. In 1996, he was cast in *Scream*—a low-budget thriller that would change his life.

What a Scream!

Scream was written by Kevin Williamson, an unknown with a great idea for a new film. Kevin's idea for a teen slasher flick was originally called *Scary Movie*, but the folks at Miramax thought that sounded too much like a comedy, so the title was changed to *Scream*. To ensure that *Scream* would be a truly frightening flick, the Miramax team decided to hire Wes Craven, king of the creepy movies, to direct. But even though Craven was a well-known entity in the horror world, Miramax wasn't so sold on the film that they would grant it a big budget. They allotted only fifteen million dollars in their annual budget toward the making of *Scream*.

In part to save money, the cast of *Scream* featured very few big-name stars. (Drew Barrymore was the only established young Hollywood actor in the cast—and she was killed off in the first twenty minutes! The other big name, Henry Winkler, was best known as Fonzie in *Happy Days*, which had been a hit almost twenty years before.) But somehow, having a cast of unknowns worked to make the film even scarier to the millions of teens who flocked to the theaters to see it again and again. By the beginning of 1997, however, none of the actors involved with *Scream* (Matt, Neve Campbell, and Skeet Ulrich) would ever be called unknown again.

Not that *Scream* was a huge hit in the beginning. The film was released during the Christmas holiday season—a move that could have been disastrous, according to traditional Hollywood wisdom. Christmas is considered a happy time, when families flock to joyous PG-rated family fare. An R-rated slasher is not the kind of thing most studios release in December.

At first, it looked like the naysayers were

going to be right. In its opening weekend, *Scream* earned only three million dollars at the box office. That's not much cash, especially considering that it was the profitable holiday season. So when it came to the topic of *Scream*, there were no ho-ho-hos at Miramax. It looked like *Scream* was going to be a disaster.

But then a sort of Christmas movie miracle occurred. Word of mouth started spreading. The kids who actually had seen *Scream* thought it was, well, a scream! And they told their pals to see it. Suddenly, the numbers started going up, and up, and up. In the end, *Scream* earned 161 million dollars worldwide—and spawned a sequel, *Scream 2*. (*Scream 3* is currently in production.)

Matthew was not in *Scream 2*, having been killed off at the end of *Scream*, but he was able to parlay his newfound fame as a homicidal maniac into a multifaceted career.

He's the Boss

With a hit like *Scream* on his résumé, Matthew suddenly found himself getting scripts from anyone who was anyone in Hollywood. But Matthew was no longer hungry, and he could finally afford to take on only those roles that interested him. And those were often in smaller independent films.

One of those films was *The Curve*, in which Matt played yet another mentally unstable character, Tim, who believes a rumor that a college student will automatically get an A if his or her roommate commits suicide. So, rather than waste a lot of time studying, Tim plots to kill one of his roommates and make it look like a suicide.

The Curve was one of the big success stories of the 1998 Sundance Film Festival, and was eventually sold to Trimark Pictures for a price that was "in the high seven figures," according to Matthew.

While Matt loves acting, the role he feels most comfortable in is actually behind the scenes, as a film producer. In 1999, Matt bought the rights to a script called *Spanish Judges* for one dollar (plus a piece of the profits) from writer William Rehor. Matt decided to star in as well as produce the story of a schemer who takes advantage of a weird couple played by Valeria Golino and Vincent D'Onofrio.

"I went out to put it together because I believed in it so much," he says.

Producing *Spanish Judges* changed Matt's opinion of the business of filmmaking. "Actors love to blame the producer," he explains. "Not enough time. Not enough money. You blame the producer. [My] eyes have been opened."

Matthew followed up his producing debut with an acting role in 1999's *S.L.C. Punk!* He played Stevo, the leader of a group of boys who rebel against the uptight Salt Lake City (S.L.C.) establishment in the 1980s by going punk—in dress, music, and attitude.

Stevo may have been slightly self-absorbed, but he had nothing on Matt's next character, Brock Hudson, a fictional alumnus of MTV's *The Real World*, in the comedy feature *She's All That*. Brock may not have been a killer, like some of Matt's other characters, but he definitely was, to put it mildly, a total jerk.

She's All That was a big teen fave, and it proved to be a breakthrough role for its star, Freddie Prinze, Jr. Matt and Freddie may not have been best buds on the screen ("enemies" is more the way you might describe the relationship between their two characters), but in real life the two did develop a great off-screen friendship. And in August of 1999, when Freddie won *Seventeen* magazine's Teen Choice Award for choice actor in a film, he made sure to thank Matt for the part he played in the success of *She's All That*. The two also shared screen time in the science fiction/action flick *Wing Commander*. Matt's character was nicknamed Maniac. (No big shock there!)

Matt loves to surprise his audiences by bringing something new and unexpected to each of his roles. His next choice was something his fans could never have predicted. He played Longaville in *Love's Labour's Lost*, a musical comedy based on William Shakespeare's play. The movie was directed by Kenneth Branagh, who is well known for his brilliant interpretations of the Bard's best. *Love's Labour's Lost*, which completed production in late 1999, had a stellar cast, including Kenneth Branagh, Alicia Silverstone, and Nathan Lane.

A *Scream* star doing Shakespeare? What will Matt think of next?

Matt's Next Move

It's hard to say what kind of role Matt will take on next. He knows that playing psychos is what he is best known for, but he is keenly aware that he needs to show that he can do more. So don't expect him to keep up that maniacal persona forever.

"For me, it's an interesting challenge trying to maintain a balance in a career," he says.

But being balanced doesn't mean constantly being the lead man in big-budget, high-profile flicks. "I don't want to be a big Hollywood star . . . I did not get into the business of acting to become rich, powerful, and famous," he insists.

Matt is getting famous despite himself. In 1999, he made it to *Entertainment Weekly*'s cool "it" list, a survey of the hottest players in Hollywood. According to the magazine, Matt was chosen for his performance as "the poignant punk revolutionist Stevo in the recent *S.L.C. Punk!* Lillard moves from mere *Scream* teen to seasoned performer."

Look for Matt to be working behind the cameras more often as the years go by. He's already slated to produce a movie called *The Collector* ("a project I love," he declares) as well as to direct the low-budget *Robin Dingo*, in which he may also star.

With a schedule like that, where will Matt ever get the time for romance? He says that if the right woman came around, he'd make the time. Matt's last big romance was with his *Scream* costar Neve Campbell, which caused a bit of a scandal, since she was still married at the time. (She's now divorced.) Although the two have since broken up, they remain good buds, and Matt says she's one of the most considerate people he knows.

The girl who does eventually grab Matt's heart is in for a wonderful relationship. He may play a homicidal maniac on the screen, but in real life, Matt is a totally romantic guy.

Nancy Krulik

"I love sending and getting flowers," he told *Teen* magazine.

Now that the word is out, florists all over America better be prepared. These days, It Boy Matthew Lillard has millions of female fans. And now that they know the way to his heart, business is sure to be booming.

120

Fast Facts

Full name: Matthew Lyn Lillard
Birthday: January 24, 1970
Astrological sign: Aquarius
Siblings: A younger sister, Amy
Pets: A German shorthaired pointer mix named Mirth
Favorite musicians: The Notorious B.I.G. and Wu-Tang Clan
Dislikes: Slackers and pessimists
Hobbies: Playing chess and Dungeons and Dragons
Secret fears: Getting fat and having bad breath

Tobey Maguire
A Wonder Boy's Rise to Fame

For years, Tobey Maguire was definitely the best actor nobody had ever heard of. As you can imagine, it is that way with a lot of actors who take on supporting roles. Their great contribution is never fully recognized—although you'd surely miss it if it weren't there. But these days, Tobey is getting his due, appearing in three of 1999's most fascinating films, *Wonder Boys*, *Ride with the Devil*, and *The Cider House Rules*. It seems that in the new millennium, the actor best known for being Leonardo DiCaprio's real-life sidekick is finally becoming famous on his own.

Of course, that doesn't mean that the media is giving up on Tobey's F.O.L. (Friend of Leo) status. After all, the two have been buds since childhood, when they met on the set of Leo's TV series, *Parenthood*. The boys became fast friends off-screen, and later Tobey played Leo's sidekick on-screen as Chuck Bolger in *This Boy's Life*.

He worked with Leonardo again when the two were all grown up, in the controversial film *Don's Plum*. (Don't be shocked if you've never heard of *Don's Plum*; it was a small film made as a favor for a friend that has never been released. Both Leo and Tobey have gone through a lot of legal maneuvering to ensure that the film never sees the light of day. The two actors say the film was made as a favor, and was never intended to be a full-length feature release.)

Interviewer after interviewer has asked Tobey what it's like to travel in Leo's posse, especially since Tobey, unlike most of Leo's buds, doesn't smoke or drink. But Tobey is a loyal friend. He's not spilling any beans on Leo.

"At an interview once, this guy had pages and pages of questions about him. If people want to do an article about Leo, they should call him," he recently sternly told an interviewer from *Cosmopolitan* magazine.

But Tobey did say that being friendly with *Titanic*'s It Boy did help prepare him for the megastardom he seems poised for himself.

"I've watched Leo go through his stuff, and I

think he's done a good job," Tobey says. "I think it's really a test of who you are. Especially for someone on that level and with what happened to him. It's disheartening what people do. But you just shrug it off and laugh at it and go."

Is Tobey up to the tests of stardom? He's certainly about to find out.

A $100 Bribe

Tobey Maguire was born on June 27, 1975. To say that he had a rocky childhood would definitely be an understatement. His parents split when he was very young, and Tobey was passed from relative's house to relative's house, sharing space with (depending on the year) his mom and her boyfriend, his mom and her sister, his grandmother, his father, and his father and stepmother.

"I lived in so many situations" is the way Tobey describes his early childhood.

Tobey didn't know it at the time, but all that moving around was preparing him for life as an actor. "I was very malleable," he told *Premiere* magazine of those early years. "I would direct myself in how I was going to fit in the quickest way, wherever we were."

When Tobey was young, he dreamed of being a chef like his father. But his mother had other plans for her adorable little boy. Tobey's mother had grown up as the daughter of a construction worker for the Disney company. Her dad worked on a lot of film sets, as well as having built some of the rides at Disneyland. When she was a young girl, Tobey's mom had wanted to audition for the Mickey Mouse Club's troupe of kid stars, the Mousketeers. But her father wouldn't let her.

When she became a mom herself, Tobey's mother encouraged her son to try the career she'd never had a chance to pursue. Tobey didn't seem to show any interest in the world of lights, cameras, and action, but Tobey's mom wasn't one to give up. So when Tobey was in eighth grade, she offered him a hundred dollars to take a drama course instead of home economics (where Tobey wanted to take cooking lessons to be a chef like his dad) in school.

"Maybe I was supposed to be her Mousketeer or something," Tobey jokes.

Tobey decided to take the money and run. He began auditioning for commercials, TV, film—anything that he was called for. His first job was an ad for McDonald's. Later on, he did more commercial work, including one for Doritos tortilla chips, which Tobey says he'll never forget.

"I remember doing this Doritos commercial where there were four days in a row of eating them," he recalled in *Details* magazine. "I will tell you I have not eaten many Doritos since."

Soon, Tobey moved from TV commercials to guest spots on TV shows. Look closely and you can spot a young Tobey on reruns of everything from *Roseanne* to *Blossom* (on which his character was named simply Boy) to *Walker, Texas Ranger*.

Tobey's big break came in 1992, when he was seventeen. He was given the title role of Scott Melrod in the then-fledgling Fox network's new sitcom *Great Scott!*

The series' run was a total disaster. The cast filmed thirteen episodes, but the network only ran six of them. It wasn't that *Great Scott!* was a bad show. It's just that it was on on Sunday nights, up against CBS's long-standing news powerhouse *60 Minutes. Great Scott!* never had a chance. "It was on right before the *Ben Stiller Show*; everybody remembers that one," Tobey joked to *Premiere* magazine.

Not that he's bitter or anything.

Makin' Movies

After the *Great Scott!* fiasco, Tobey wandered around Hollywood for a while. He worked on *This Boy's Life* and on a small film called *Revenge of the Red Baron,* and added his talent to made-for-TV movies like *Spoils of War, A Child's*

Cry for Help, and *Seduced by Madness.* Those jobs paid the bills, but that was about it. Stardom seemed pretty far from his grasp.

In 1995, Tobey took a role in a short film called *Duke of Groove.* The film went on to win an Oscar in the best short film category. Being part of the cast was an honor for Tobey, but it did little for his career, since so few people ever get to see short films. Tobey was still hunting for the role that would get him noticed by both the Hollywood community and the world.

He found what he was searching for in 1997. That year, Tobey had supporting roles in two highly anticipated films. The first, *The Ice Storm,* told the story of two emotionally uptight (you might even say *icy*) Connecticut families. Tobey played Paul, a prep-school boy who plays it cool, while really being a sad, scared kid inside. *Premiere* magazine praised Tobey for his performance in the film, saying "Maguire's charm is that he can swing easily between . . . the cool cat with the canary in his mouth, and the rejected kid."

Tobey's second film in 1997 was Woody Allen's *Deconstructing Harry,* in which he played Harvey Stern. Tobey was thrilled to have been cast in the role by Woody Allen himself.

Being in a Woody Allen film guarantees an actor ink in the magazines and trade papers. Suddenly, Tobey was a hot commodity. The press was knocking at his door, wanting to interview him, and find out what made him tick as an actor.

Tobey had a surprisingly candid answer for the reporters. "I don't have that 'too cool' attitude about acting," he explained in *Vanity Fair.* "It's a job, and I have to pay the rent."

Tobey had no trouble keeping his landlord happy in the year that followed. He started out 1998 by making a cameo appearance in the highly acclaimed *Fear and Loathing in Las Vegas.* "I played this really weird hitchhiker who has long blond hair. They bleached my eyebrows for it and they had to shave me completely bald to put the wig on," he recalls.

Tobey's next film put him in the hot seat—as one of the main characters in the big-budget flick *Pleasantville.* It was Tobey's first time on the set of a big-budget film, and although Reese Witherspoon was the big-name draw, Tobey knew that, as one of the leads, a lot of the responsibility lay on his shoulders as well. He figured that out one afternoon when he was feeling very run-down during the shoot. As he told *People* Online: "The moment that I felt that was . . . when [director] Gary Ross came up to me and said, 'Okay, Tobey, how are you feeling?' I was really tired that day and I said, 'I'm pretty tired.' He said, 'I'm only going to say this once, and I don't want you to feel pressured, but I want you to understand the importance of it. This is a $40-million movie, and it pretty much rests on your shoulders.' "

You can bet Tobey went to bed early that night.

But the truth was, Tobey wasn't the real star of *Pleasantville*. None of the actors were.

"The film is the star," he says. "I knew that going into it. It's an ensemble movie and the concept of the film itself is more the star of the film than any actors are."

Tobey's *Pleasantville* character, David, was a complex one. Like Tobey, David came from a broken home, and often found himself disengaged from what was going on in his household. But unlike the then-twenty-three-year-old Tobey, David was a teenager, which meant that Tobey had to reach back into his past to understand why David reacted to certain situations the way he did.

"I wouldn't want to be playing teenagers ten years from now," he admitted to *People* Online at the time, "but for now, it's fine. I can still relate. I'm not too far away. Although it's interesting because I'm finding I look at kids and I can't quite tell what age they are when they are like thirteen, fourteen, or fifteen . . . I'm starting to get removed from it."

In the film, Tobey and his sister (played by Reese Witherspoon) are zapped into their TV

Nancy Krulik

and find themselves part of their favorite 1950s rerun sitcom. The brother-and-sister duo then bring a little 1990s "color" into the tightly wound 1950s world.

Throughout the filming, Tobey and Reese developed a relationship that was very much like a real-life sibling thing—rivalry included.

"We got to hang out together about three months before filming started," Reese explains. "By the time we started shooting, we had the bickering down pat, and we knew exactly how irritated to be with each other. As the movie went on, I felt like we built that dynamic and became more like brother and sister."

Tobey agrees, saying, "It was a really important experience for me to work with Reese."

Pleasantville's offbeat theme hit a chord with moviegoers, and with critics. The film did well at the box office, adding to Tobey's newly developed star power.

Hollywood's Wonder Boy

In 1999, acclaimed *L.A. Confidential* director Curtis Hanson was busy beginning production on his new film, *Wonder Boys*. The film had a wonderful pedigree behind it. Besides having Hanson at the helm, the script was written by Steve Kloves, who had written *The Fabulous Baker Boys*. Michael Douglas had already agreed to play the leading role of a middle-aged professor and novelist who fails to live up to the potential he had displayed in his youth. Douglas's pregnant lover was to be played by *Fargo*'s Oscar-winning Frances McDormand.

James Leer was different from any character Tobey had brought to the screen. He was a college student, coming of age in both a social and an intellectual context. He was also a depressed misfit.

"It [was] a scary character to play," Tobey recalls. "You don't want to ham it up, but you still want it to be funny. He's a spooky kind of funny."

After filming a demanding movie like *Wonder Boys*, some actors would take a break, maybe go on an extended holiday. But not Tobey. He jumped right into his next film, *Ride with the Devil*, a Civil War drama directed by *The Ice Storm*'s Ang Lee and based on the novel *Woe to Live On* by Daniel Woodrell.

The film, which was the story of a band of guerrilla fighters on the Kansas-Missouri border during the Civil War, starred *Scream*'s Skeet Ulrich as Tobey's best friend. But the film got most of its publicity because it also starred pop singer Jewel in her acting debut. Jewel played a love interest that comes between Tobey's character and Skeet's.

"It's actually very sad," Tobey says of the film.

"There's the Kansas Jaywalkers and the Missouri Bushwhackers. And it's guerrilla warfare. Basically, people come and kill your family, and burn your house to the ground, and you have nowhere else to go. So you just sort of ride alone, and you want vengeance. The film is about a lot of things. There's battles and love stories and friendships and emancipation in many forms."

Ride with the Devil required its actors to spend long hours in the hot sun, and to perform stunts that they were not used to doing on an average film. Tobey jumped into the hard work head-on, staying true to his credo that there is almost nothing he wouldn't do for the sake of a film—except smoke cigarettes. Tobey has already kicked that habit, and he never wants to be tempted to go back to it again.

After the arduous *Ride with the Devil* shoot, Tobey kept on working, this time taking on the role of Homer Wells in *The Cider House Rules*. The film was directed by Lasse Halström—who had directed Tobey's pal Leo's Oscar-nominated performance in *What's Eating Gilbert Grape*—and was based on the novel by John Irving. In *The Cider House Rules*, Tobey plays Homer Wells, an orphan who ventures out into the world in search of new life experiences. Homer's journeys allow him to meet fascinating characters, including an army pilot (played by

Clueless's Paul Rudd) who takes him under his wing and a beautiful migrant worker (played by singer Erykah Badu in her acting debut).

Kicking Back

By the time *Wonder Boys*, *Ride with the Devil*, and *The Cider House Rules* hit the screen, even Tobey the workaholic had to acknowledge that he needed a break from acting in front of the cameras.

"To be honest with you, I'm not necessarily in favor of working all that much," he told *Cosmopolitan* of his decision to make three films back-to-back. "But they've been really great roles, so I couldn't say no."

These days, Tobey is looking at scripts and planning his next move. He's also heavily into relaxing through yoga, which he does twenty minutes every day. And although he still spends some nights partying with his old pal Leo, Tobey's more likely to be found hanging out with his girlfriend, whose name he would prefer to keep private.

"I'm just trying to learn this whole press thing," he explained to *Cosmopolitan*. "What to protect and what to be open about."

What Tobey will say is that he is very romantic. He talks to his lady at least once every day, no matter where he is. And when he was on location and had to miss her birthday, he sent her a letter and a bouquet of gardenias. During his work-related travels, he sets up pictures of his girlfriend right near his bed.

And you thought guys like that only existed in the movies!

The Future

Tobey's goals for the future are simple. He just wants to continue being part of great films. Unlike many Hollywood types, Tobey feels that being the lead character doesn't matter at all. He just wants his work to be wonderful, and for the films he makes to send a message to their audience.

So does Tobey think he's ready for superstardom?

"I don't know," he admits honestly. "I'm just sort of going along for the ride. These doors have opened, and I'm just gonna see what happens. So I guess I am ready for it!"

Fast Facts

Full name: Tobias Vincent Maguire

Birthday: June 27, 1975

Astrological sign: Cancer

Parents: Vincent and Wendy

Favorite musical artists: Beck, the Beastie Boys, Led Zeppelin, the Cure

Favorite foods: Tobey is a vegetarian

Favorite sport: Basketball

Actors he most sees himself resembling: "I think I am going somewhere between Tom Hanks and John Malkovich."

Ewan McGregor
A New Breed of Jedi

It's a little-known fact that Ewan McGregor had been a part of the *Star Wars* saga long before he took on the role of Obi-Wan Kenobi in *Star Wars: Episode I—The Phantom Menace*. In fact, back in the 1970s, when the original trilogy was produced, he'd "played" the role of both Han Solo and Luke Skywalker.

As a kid, Ewan, like everyone else on the planet, was caught up in the *Star Wars* legacy. "I used to know every word in *Star Wars*," he told *TV Guide* of his fascination with the first film he ever saw. "Me and my friends used to act out all the parts."

Okay, so maybe acting out a laser battle in your backyard isn't the same as being part of an actual George Lucas *Star Wars* extravaganza, but it was the beginning of Ewan's force-filled career. So you can imagine his excitement when he walked on the set of *The Phantom Menace* and practically bumped into one of the stars from the original trilogy of *Star Wars* films.

"When I met R2-D2 for the first time, I almost went down to the ground," he recalls excitedly of the first time he came face-to-face (well, actually, face-to-knee) with the little round robot. "I saw [it] and I just started screaming. All the prop-makers turned around and nodded. They all knew how I felt."

Being a huge *Star Wars* fan made Ewan even more dedicated to getting the part of Obi-Wan just right. And that wasn't easy. After all, in the original films, the part of Obi-Wan Kenobi was played by veteran award-winning actor Alec Guinness. His memory was etched in the minds of millions of dedicated *Star Wars* fans, of which Ewan considers himself a member.

But although he tried in some ways to blend his voice and speech patterns with those Alec Guinness gave the character ("He's got this very specific older man's voice," Ewan explained to reporters shortly after he'd been cast in the role. "It would be great if I could trace it back to his youth and get it right."), Ewan didn't try to do an exact imitation of the young Alec.

"It's hard enough to walk into a film that is

expected to live up to the glory of the previous *Star Wars* movies. I don't want people comparing me to Alec Guinness, because he's one of the greats. I can only be me and hope that people appreciate my work."

When *The Phantom Menace* was released in May of 1999, that is exactly what happened. Although the film did not get stellar reviews, Ewan McGregor was a favorite with the critics and the fans. They could not wait for Ewan to get in front of the cameras again and begin filming *Star Wars: Episode II* (which will be filming in Australia throughout 2000).

Ewan's rave reviews shouldn't have come as a surprise to anyone. After all, throughout his career, he's had a habit of taking on roles and making them completely and believably his own. Of course, none of those previous parts had ever been as high-profile as *The Phantom Menace*. The movies in which he played a heroin addict *(Trainspotting)*, a nineteenth-century British flirt *(Emma)*, and an unemployed coal miner *(Brassed Off)* never drew the audiences *The Phantom Menace* did. But that kind of fame has never mattered to Ewan. In fact, for years, he's bad-mouthed Hollywood's "event" movies—big time.

"All they talk about are budgets and meetings—the last thing anybody seems to be worried about is the movie," he complains about

Hollywood bigwigs. The blockbuster he hates most is *Independence Day*, a multimillion-dollar success story that Ewan calls simply "an abomination."

Then why take on the lead role in a series of films that was certain to leave *Independence Day* in the dust?

Well, there are a lot of reasons. For starters, Ewan doesn't place *The Phantom Menace* in the same category as *Independence Day*.

"I don't think of them as event movies," he explains of the *Star Wars* flicks. "It's not like being in *RoboCop 5* or something. The *Star Wars* movies are way beyond pictures. I can't say no."

Besides, *Star Wars* movies are part of Ewan's family legacy. His uncle, actor Denis Lawson, was the only person to play an X-Wing pilot in all three of the original *Star Wars* movies.

"I'll never forget waiting for my mother to pick me up from school and taking me to see the first movie. I was six years old and very proud my uncle Denis was in it," Ewan remembers.

And he hopes to instill those memories in his own child, four-year-old Clara.

"What's great is, if things work out, my daughter will be five or six by the time all of this batch comes out. It'll be great for her to have her daddy in it, y'know," Ewan muses.

And speaking of great, that's what life is these

days for Ewan McGregor. Not only has he gotten the opportunity to play out one of his childhood fantasies, he continues to grow as an actor, taking chances in small independent films. And his family life makes him happy each and every day. Ewan is at the top of his game.

But life hasn't always been so amazing for Ewan McGregor. In fact, it wasn't so long ago that people in his hometown thought Ewan was on a downward spiral that seemed to have no end.

Growing Up

Ewan McGregor was born on March 31, 1971, in the rural town of Crieff, Scotland. There were only six thousand people in his hometown, and that was too small as far as he was concerned. Ewan was always a rebel. Even when he was a baby, his determined temper tantrums were the stuff family legends are made of.

Growing up, Ewan never had a need to dress, look, or act like anyone else just because that was what was considered normal. But sometimes, even an individualist like Ewan had a tough time expressing himself through fashion. In a small town, being different can be difficult.

"I could never be a punk or a mod," he says

of his teenage style, "because the town was too small. You'd be the only punk in town, and you'd have to hang around on the street on your own being the only punk, and that would be dreary," he explains.

So instead of hanging out on the streets by himself, Ewan watched movies. And not just *Star Wars* flicks. He loved old black-and-white films. "My favorites were from the '30s or '40s," he says. "They were unashamedly romantic. I don't like these cynical romances these days . . . Back then, it was done with so much more skill."

But spending your time watching old movies on the telly doesn't make for a great report card. In fact, Ewan's grades and attitude toward school were always a bit of a problem—not to mention an embarrassment to his father, who just happened to be the physical education teacher at the Morrison Academy, where Ewan and his older brother, Colin, went to school.

The Morrison Academy was an old-fashioned, strict school—not exactly the perfect atmosphere for creative types like Ewan. He hated putting on the school's uptight gray-and-blue uniform every morning, and sitting in most classes made him absolutely stir-crazy.

One part of the school's extracurricular program, however, excited him. Surprise! It wasn't the theater department. In fact, Ewan was hardly involved in school plays at all. Although he idolized his uncle Denis when he was a boy, and said that he was "absolutely determined" to follow in his career footsteps, Ewan was more drawn to music than dramatics during his years at Morrison. In his bedroom, he hung a huge poster of Elvis Presley, his musical idol at the time. But he modeled his hairstyle after a different kind of idol—1980s punk star Billy Idol.

Despite his love for Elvis and Billy Idol, Ewan's initial musical talents were more classical than rockabilly or punk. He actually won an award for playing the French horn. Later on, Ewan picked up some sticks and started beating on skins, as the drummer in a garage band called Scarlet Pride.

But music alone isn't going to get a kid through high school. By the time Ewan turned sixteen, his grades had plummeted, and he was absolutely miserable. And although both of his parents knew that an education was very important, they couldn't stand to see their son so miserable. Reluctantly, they decided to let Ewan drop out of school and give acting a try.

"It was a really brave decision for them to make," Ewan acknowledges gratefully. "They didn't make me feel bad about it. That was a relief."

Not that Ewan thinks dropping out of school

is good for everybody. In fact, he easily admits that not having a high school diploma has put him at a disadvantage with his own daughter. Not only is he unable to converse with Clara in her first language (Ewan's wife, Eve, is French, and she speaks to Clara in both French and in English, but mostly in French), someday he'll have trouble helping her with her English homework as well. Ewan confesses he paid so little attention in school that he can't even name all the parts of speech.

"I know roughly what an adjective is, but beyond that, I have no idea," he admits.

A School Ewan Could Relate To

"Suddenly, my horizons widened into Cinema-Scope," Ewan recalls about being let off the hook from school. Within a few weeks, he found himself a job at a local theater in nearby Perth. But Ewan wasn't on the stage; he was working behind the scenes as a stagehand. Ewan considered the repertory theater his school, and spent time learning everyone's job.

"I was a real pain in the backside because I was so keen [on learning]," he remembers.

Before long, Ewan managed to make the move from backstage to the stage itself, taking on small nonspeaking roles in shows like *A Passage to India*.

But Ewan spent only six months in Perth. He soon received a letter telling him that he had been accepted to a one-year acting course at Kircaldy College. For the first time in his life, Ewan was excited about going to school.

Ewan finished the year at Kircaldy and followed that up by enrolling in a three-year degree program at the Guildhall School of Music and Drama, one of Scotland's most prestigious schools. Ewan took his studies at both colleges seriously, memorizing mountains of dialogue and trying to learn from the seemingly endless stream of criticism from his professors.

But once again, at the age of twenty, Ewan dropped out of school—just before he could take his final exams and receive his degree. The only difference was that this time, Ewan wasn't dropping out because he was frustrated and unhappy, he was dropping out to take on a professional acting role—as the star of a TV miniseries!

Goin' Pro

Lipstick on Your Collar was a miniseries written by the British playwright Dennis Potter. Ewan had auditioned for the part of young Private Mick Hopper on a whim—he figured he needed to get experience with auditions. He never dreamed he'd actually get the part.

But he did. Ewan jumped into the role of a bored Russian translator in the British army during the 1950s. It wasn't a hard character for him to conjure up. Like Ewan, the private was a rock-and-roll rebel stuck in a conservative atmosphere. During the filming of *Lipstick on Your Collar,* Ewan got to perform an on-screen imitation of his former musical idol, Elvis Presley. "Doing him was easy," Ewan recalls. "I'd spent half my childhood imitating Elvis."

Although the miniseries received mixed reviews, Ewan was singled out by the London *Times,* which said that "Ewan McGregor was good in the part."

It wasn't wild praise, but that review was all the encouragement Ewan needed. He was more sure than ever that he was going to make it in show biz!

But success was slower in coming than he'd anticipated. In fact, there were no offers for six months following *Lipstick on Your Collar.* Being unemployed for six months can put a drain on your pocketbook. So you can imagine how psyched Ewan was when he was finally offered a small role in Robin Williams's 1993 movie *Being Human.* Robin Williams was already an established star. It seemed like everything Robin touched turned to gold. Ewan was ready for his breakthrough.

But that breakthrough was going to have to

wait. By the time the picture made it to the screen, Ewan had only two lines—and hardly anybody heard them, because *Being Human* wound up being one of Robin Williams's few box-office bombs.

But Ewan didn't give up. He jumped right back on his acting horse and tried and tried again. He took a small role as a page in an English production of *What the Butler Saw* to tide him over until a larger role came his way.

In 1994, Ewan's prayers for a showcase role came true. He was cast in the lead of a BBC miniseries called *Scarlet & Black*. He played Julien Sorel, a French carpenter who tries to be like his idol, Napoleon, by becoming part of French high society.

Almost one million viewers caught Ewan's performance in *Scarlet & Black*—and lots of those viewers were teenage girls. Suddenly, he was getting tons of fan mail. Ewan's hot looks and sexy bedroom eyes were just what teenagers throughout England were looking for. Ironically, those same looks were a problem for Britain's film critics. The London daily *Mirror* actually complained that Ewan was a "far too devastatingly handsome toy-boy [to play] Julien."

Oh, come on! Who ever heard of being too handsome?

Getting bad reviews was painful for Ewan,

but learning to ignore the critics is a lesson every actor has to learn at some time. And he took comfort in the fact that he had attracted a whole new crowd of fans—of the female persuasion. Besides, before long, Ewan would be able to show those naysaying critics a thing or two!

Hopping on the Train

Even with the bad reviews, Ewan's star was on the rise. Suddenly, scripts were coming to him for review. There was one part he says he will be forever grateful to have accepted, that of an accused rapist in a TV series called *Kavanagh QC*. The series itself wasn't very memorable to the viewing public, but it's one Ewan will never forget, because he met his wife, Eve Mavrakis, on the set.

Eve was a production designer on the series. Ewan says that when he saw her, it was "love at first sight." The attraction was obviously mutual. Ewan and Eve married a year later, in 1995. The wedding was like something you read about in fairy-tale books—the two said their vows on a villa in rural France, surrounded by sunflowers. The funny part was that the entire ceremony was in French, and Ewan had no idea what he was promising. But he did pledge his love to Eve with a simple *oui*.

Another role that caught Ewan's fancy in 1994 was in a low-budget thriller called *Shallow Grave*.

Taking on a part in a low-budget film after finally getting through to the masses may seem like one of the dumbest career choices of all time, but Ewan has never been one to do things the way the establishment sees fit. Throughout his career, Ewan has made his choices based on his heart, not on his pocketbook or the advice of agents and managers. When Ewan finds a script he likes, he's in.

"I'm just into making quality stuff if I can, with interesting people and good scripts," he explains.

According to Ewan, *Shallow Grave* fit both criteria. Not only was the thriller well written and the characters multidimensional, but working with director Danny Boyle helped Ewan discover just what a great actor he could be. And for that, Ewan says, he will always be grateful.

"I really just want to make films with Danny Boyle," Ewan claims. "I'm never happier working with anyone else. He makes films the way I think they should be made. He gets my best work. I don't know how or why, but I'm not as good with anyone else."

To everyone's surprise (except Ewan and Danny's), *Shallow Grave* was a box-office success—becoming the number one movie of 1994 in England. That gave Ewan new clout in the movie biz. But, more important, *Shallow Grave* provided Ewan with an artistic ally in Danny Boyle. Both men were more interested in making good movies than in making profitable ones—something almost unheard of in show-biz.

Danny and Ewan worked together again in 1996, in the film *Trainspotting*, which depicted the lives of a group of heroin addicts, led by Ewan. Ewan took several months to prepare for his role as addict Mark Renton. He dieted ferociously and dropped twenty-eight pounds to give himself the almost skeletal look desperate junkies take on. He met with heroin addicts and rehab doctors to learn about what addiction feels like. However, that's as far as Ewan would go to research his role. Despite persistent rumors in the press, Ewan swears he never tried heroin as part of his preparation for the part. In fact, he has never done drugs at all. Even those realistic needle scenes in the film were completely fake.

Trainspotting was a dark, depressing look at what drugs can do to young people—not exactly an uplifting theatrical experience. But it was one folks were drawn to in droves. Eventually, the little independent film, which cost two and a half million dollars to make, earned seventy million dollars worldwide. It was the most profitable movie of 1996, according to *Variety*.

Ewan turned his *Trainspotting* success into a launching pad for more movies. He went to work on more independent features, including *Brassed Off* and the period drama *Emma*, a film that Ewan believes was a huge mistake on his part. "I never even read the [Jane Austen] book," he says of his lack of preparation for his supporting role as the flirtatious Frank Churchill. "I was particularly awful in that one."

No doubt about it, if Ewan has one addiction, it's work. In 1997, he continued his nonstop working streak, taking on roles in six more independent films, including another Danny Boyle collaboration, *A Life Less Ordinary*, which costarred Cameron Diaz as Ewan's romantic interest.

He also had a turn as Duncan Stewart, a convenience store gunman who holds Nurse Hathaway (Julianna Margulies) captive on an episode of the mega-popular TV drama *ER*. The role earned Ewan an Emmy nomination for best guest appearance. Ewan loved working with the *ER* cast, and was extremely proud of his performance, but by the end of 1997, the stress of his success was beginning to show.

"I love the movies, and I've had a hard time

saying no," he told one reporter in 1998. "I have to learn to pace myself."

People close to Ewan say that he had every intention of slowing down. But then an offer came that Ewan could not refuse.

Star-dom

George Lucas told *GQ* magazine that he cast Ewan as the young Obi-Wan Kenobi in *The Phantom Menace* because, of all the people who screen-tested for the role, "he came out the best. The chemistry was there with the other cast members, and he gave his heart and soul."

There's nothing new there. Ewan always gives his heart and soul to his parts (well, maybe, except for *Emma*'s Frank Churchill).

Ewan first heard he had gotten the part of Obi-Wan Kenobi while he was on the set of another movie, *Velvet Goldmine*. "I got a call in the morning. I was told I had the part, but I wasn't allowed to tell anyone for a month and a half," he remembers. "It was quite a day." (Just for the record, Ewan did leak the news to his wife and his parents—who were sworn to secrecy at the time!)

Ironically, taking the part in *Star Wars* meant that Ewan had to give up the leading-man status he'd built up in his independent film career. Suddenly, he was cast in the role of a Jedi apprentice, making him the sidekick to Liam Neeson's Qui-Gon Jinn, the Jedi master. But if Ewan's fans were disappointed that their hero didn't have a larger role, they could easily take solace in the knowledge that Ewan would be the master and Anakin Skywalker the apprentice in *Episode II*.

There was no way Ewan could have predicted or prepared for the onslaught of fame that his *Star Wars* role brought. And although he was crazy about the original series when he was a boy, he was genuinely shocked by how much the film meant to fans of the *Star Wars* series— particularly the adult fans.

" 'May the force be with you!' People are actually saying that to me," he told a reporter for *GQ* soon after the release of *The Phantom Menace*. "I think that's quite batty."

In the month before *The Phantom Menace*'s May 1999 release, Ewan's face seemed to be everywhere. There wasn't an entertainment magazine known to mankind that didn't have his big blue eyes staring out from the cover.

"When I saw [my face on the cover of *Entertainment Weekly*], I thought, I've really made it now," he told a reporter for *TNT Rough Cut*. "I'm very much aware of this extraordinary position I'm in; to be working, making films that I am passionate about."

What's Next for Ewan?

For the time being, Ewan's future seems to be tied up in a galaxy far, far away. He will be spending most of 2000 in Sydney, filming the next *Star Wars* installment. But he won't be lonely there. Although he took his *Star Wars* check and bought a home in London with "a big garden" for his daughter, Clara, to play in, Ewan makes it a practice to bring his wife and daughter along with him on his movie shoots whenever possible. Ewan, who remains very close to his parents and his brother, feels that a family should stick together.

Unlike other *Star Wars* veterans, like Mark Hamill and Carrie Fisher, who will be forever associated with their roles of Luke Skywalker and Princess Leia, Ewan has no fear that he will be remembered solely for his *Star Wars* work. "I'll keep doing other things," he explains. One of those "other things" includes the 2000 release *Moulin Rouge,* a film Ewan squeezed in between *Star Wars* films that costars Nicole Kidman.

Characteristically, Ewan has taken to using his newfound fame to help others less fortunate. He uses his celebrity status to help the homeless when he takes part in the worldwide Comic Relief effort. He plans to continue being part of Britain's red nose (as in clown) campaign for the cause.

One place you won't find Ewan, however, is making the rounds of the late-night talk shows. He simply can't stand being interviewed by the likes of David Letterman and Jay Leno.

"I don't like the way [David Letterman] interviews people. Same with Leno. Always showing people up. Really successful Hollywood movie stars cringing in their seats at the mercy of these rather arrogant and uninteresting men," he declares.

Oh, and that's another thing. Ewan has no intention of curbing his outspoken behavior just because he's become an international star.

And maybe that's what makes Ewan so lovable. There's no fear that he will ever go Hollywood. No matter how famous he gets, Ewan will always remain the kid from Crieff who wanted to be a punk rocker but didn't want to wind up standing all alone on the street.

Fast Facts

Full name: Ewan Gordon McGregor
Nickname: Ew (pronounced "you")
Birthday: March 31, 1971
Astrological sign: Aries
Parents: James and Carol
Brother: Colin
Wife: Eve
Daughter: Clara Mathilde
Hobby: Golf
Favorite band: Oasis
Favorite TV show: *ER*
Secret wish: To own a motorcycle team

Kel Mitchell
He's All That and More

Ask Kel Mitchell what he remembers about his elementary school years during the 1980s in Chicago, Illinois, and he'll probably say he mostly recalls getting into trouble. Kel was the ultimate class clown—even going so far as to do cartwheels across the classroom to reach the garbage can, or jump up to dance in the middle of math. Anything to get attention. Unfortunately, Kel didn't care if that attention was negative or positive.

"My mom was saying, 'This boy is a little too creative. I have to get him into something before he gets into trouble,'" he recalls. "So she put me into theater classes."

Theater classes were just the thing Kel needed. He remembers the first time his acting teacher asked him to go onstage and try a little improvisation.

"I didn't even know what 'improv' meant," Kel explains. "So he told me to just get up there and do stuff. I got up on the stage and I don't think I came down for like an hour . . . I was like, 'Wow! That's the stuff that's been getting me in trouble in school.' "

And it's just that improv "stuff" that has turned Kel into the number one physical comic of his generation!

Chicago's Child

From the moment he took to the stage for the first time, Kel knew that he had found a home. He was born to perform. Now all he had to do was convince casting directors of that fact.

Kel continued working with his drama teacher while he went on auditions in the Chicago metropolitan area. At first, he found roles in small community theater productions on Chicago's South Side. Then, after a while, he moved to larger shows in the downtown section of the city. That's when Kel realized that his career was going to take off.

"When you go downtown [in Chicago] it's like if you're in New York and you're going to Broadway. After that, I got an agent, and started going on like a million auditions."

One of those auditions was for a pilot for a new Nickelodeon variety comedy show called *All That*.

You Call That an Audition?

To say that Kel's audition for *All That* went smoothly would be lying, to say the least. In fact, at first, the audition was a complete disaster.

Kel had been told to prepare a funny monologue. Like any good actor, he'd come up with some pretty funny routines to dazzle the directors with. But, on the day of the audition, Kel had two tests at school. So by the time he arrived at the audition site, his brain was totally fried.

"I forgot my monologue when I went in there. And I was all embarrassed," he recalled in *Rough Cut*. "[The casting directors] were like, 'Would you like to go out and catch your breath?' So I left the room."

Kel later found out that the casting directors were so disappointed in his performance that they had already given up on Kel. They had no plans to even tape his audition. But then Kel came back in the room and tripped over a camera cable. The casting directors started laughing hysterically.

"They thought it was part of my skit," Kel remembers. "That made me feel a little bit more comfortable."

After that, Kel was able to relax and be his own wacky self. He did his stand-up routine, which included some material by veteran comedian Richard Pryor as well as some of his own jokes.

"We just had a lot of fun," Kel recalls.

So much fun, in fact, that Kel got the job. And before he knew it, he was taping the pilot episode of *All That*.

Meeting Kenan

Although Kel had developed a reputation in the Chicago theater community, he was far less experienced than some of the other *All That* cast members, especially one actor in particular, who had just come off the set of two hit Disney movies, *D2: The Mighty Ducks* and *D3: The Mighty Ducks*. His name was Kenan Thompson.

The way Kenan and Kel work together today, you would think that they had known each other for years. But Kenan and Kel did not meet until 1995, when *All That* went into production.

Kenan and Kel never planned on being partners for their skits on *All That*, but the casting directors for the show recalled that both boys had done old man characters in their audition tapes.

"I did Bill Cosby as an old man, and I think Kel did an old man in his, and that's how they put us together in a sketch called Mavis and Clavis," Kenan recalls of the first act the guys did together. "We really had the chemistry, and hit it off!"

Did they ever! Before long, Kenan and Kel were the most recognizable members of the *All That* cast. Mavis and Clavis cracked up the audience every time they appeared. So did Kenan and Kel's other characters, like Kel's Pizza Face and Coach Kreeton (who was based on two of Kel's teachers back in Chicago) and Kenan's Superdude superhero.

But of all Kel's characters, perhaps the most popular is Ed, the dreadlock-wearing, surfer-speaking counter dude at the Good Burger fast-food joint. It didn't take long for kids all over America to start repeating Ed's famous greeting, "Welcome to Good Burger, home of the Good Burger. Can I take your order?"

"Ed's a real innocent kind of guy and just takes life as it goes," Kel says, describing his character. "He takes things really literally. Like if you came up to him and asked him for a good shake, he would literally shake you."

And the Winner Is . . .

By 1996, it was clear that kids loved Kenan and Kel. So Nickelodeon followed an age-old television tradition—spinning off a new TV show based on an existing successful show. In this case, the new show was called *Kenan & Kel*. In their new TV show, Kenan and Kel played two best friends who were, not so coincidentally, named Kenan and Kel. But the guys were nothing like their TV alter egos. For one thing, in the show, the character of Kel was a total space case, something the real-life Kel could never be called.

Kenan & Kel, which debuted in August of 1996, was a huge hit for Nickelodeon. The show was also a big boost to Kel's career. Being on a sitcom gave Kel an opportunity to really develop a character (no matter how bizarre that character might be) and to show off his acting chops. In 1997, his efforts were rewarded when he beat out veteran comic actors Garry Shandling and Robert Wuhl to win the cable Ace award for best actor in a comedy series *(Kenan & Kel)*. That same year, the *Kenan & Kel* TV series won an Ace award for best children's show.

Kel was an award-winning actor with two hit series running at the same time. Still, the fans were not satisfied. They wanted more. Kel and Kenan were glad to give them exactly what they wanted!

Welcome to *Good Burger*

In early 1997, Kel found himself on his very first movie set. He and Kenan were shooting

Good Burger, a movie based on two of their *All That* characters. Once again, Kel was playing the more-than-slightly-spacy Ed. Kenan was playing Dexter, Ed's coworker, a scheming kid who thinks he knows everything.

The movie's plot was simple. A competing fast-food joint threatens to put Good Burger out of business, and it's up to Ed and Dexter to see that that doesn't happen.

Kel was thrilled to be working on the *Good Burger* movie—and not just because it was a starring role in a major motion picture. He liked the film because he felt it would give kids something worthwhile to see during the summer.

"It's a family film," he says. "It has a lot of messages like don't judge a book by its cover. It's also funny, so you laugh while you learn something."

Kel was involved in almost every aspect of filmmaking during *Good Burger*'s production. It was his first movie, and he really wanted to learn the ropes.

"Kenan had been through it before [in the *Mighty Ducks* movies]," Kel said at the time. "This is my first movie. I'm new to the game. Kenan taught me a lot. He told me there was a lot of hurry up and wait. You could do a scene that takes fifteen hours, but in the movie it lasts only ten minutes."

Kel felt so strongly about contributing to the

movie's success that he even wrote and recorded a song, "We're All Dudes," for the movie's soundtrack.

When it came time to do a video for "We're All Dudes," there was only one man Kel wanted to direct it—Kenan. Both Kenan and Kel were enrolled in college, studying filmmaking. Kenan had taken a real shine to directing, and Kel decided to let his pal have a shot at the job.

The result was great. "We're All Dudes" went into regular rotation on MTV in the fall of 1998.

Although *Good Burger* opened to only lukewarm reviews, kids loved the movie. They just figured that the critics didn't get the joke. *Good Burger* had solid earnings, leaving the field open for other movie producers to approach Kel for roles.

Invisible . . . Not!

By 1999, Kel's career plate was getting full. Not only was he working on TV and in the movies, but he had a lot of studying to do for college. Something had to give. So he gave up his spot on the *All That* roster in order to leave room for more movies.

Kel completed his first movie role without Kenan in 1999, when he joined the incredible ensemble cast of *Mystery Men,* which included Ben Stiller, Janeane Garofalo, Hank Azaria,

Paul Reubens (formerly known as Pee-wee Herman), and William H. Macy. Kel was cast as Invisible Boy, a guy who says he can become invisible—but only if you don't look at him.

In a repeat performance from his *Good Burger* days, Kel lent his musical chops to the film's soundtrack, recording the title track, "Mystery Men."

Although Kel was on his own, he was definitely not splitting from his buddy Kenan. In 1999, the two continued to work together on *Kenan & Kel,* and filmed cameo appearances as themselves in the heavily hyped *The Adventures of Rocky and Bullwinkle* movie.

Looking Toward the Future

These days, Kel Mitchell is red hot! And he is ready to take advantage of the situation. He and Kenan are already in planning to bring out their own line of clothing.

"We'll probably call it Chi-lanta," Kel says, "because I'm from Chicago and he's from Atlanta. We're still going to keep the comedy in it, like having a pocket by the knee or something."

He and Kenan are also looking to put their film school knowledge to use by possibly creating their own production company. But they don't plan on working with one another exclusively.

"[Kel] is going to venture off and do his

music thing and I'm going to do my screen-writing thing," Kenan says. "That way we give each other space so we don't fight and break up the duo over some dumb stuff. You might see him in front of the camera in a movie and see my name producing or directing."

Kel's "music thing," as Kenan puts it, includes writing his own rap songs and performing with his band, M.A.F.T.

As for his personal life, Kel has a steady relationship with a woman whose name he prefers to keep private. That's the one part of his life he prefers to keep out of the limelight.

In many ways, Kel has remained the same sweet (if extremely energetic) kid he was back when he lived in Chicago. "Where I come from, they'll beat your head until it gets back to the normal size," he jokes. Nothing much has changed about him. Well, except for one thing. Kel no longer eats hamburgers from fast-food joints. *Good Burger* put an end to that.

Fast Facts

Full Name: Kel Johari Rice Mitchell
Birthday: August 25, 1978
Astrological sign: Virgo
Mother: Meridith Mitchell
Sisters: Keyana and Kyra
Pets: A dog named Dizzy and a turtle named Imani
Favorite food: Spaghetti
Favorite movies: *Soul Food* and *The Last Dragon*
Favorite color: Red

Scott Speedman
Canada's Coolest Export

Who does Scott Speedman have to thank for his brilliant acting career? The caped crusader himself—Batman!

It's true. Even though Scott lived in Toronto, Canada, rather than in Gotham City, it was Batman who got Scott his start in acting, and saved him from years of trying to figure out what to do with his life.

While he was still in high school, Scott took a dare and went on a Canadian public access television show called *Speaker's Forum*. *Speaker's Forum* gave regular folks (which Scott was at the time) the opportunity to speak out on any subject of his choice. Scott decided to use his fifteen minutes of fame to suggest that the producers of *Batman Forever*, who were in Toronto at the time, consider him for the role of Robin in the film.

"My girlfriend at the time dared me to do it," he recalls. "I was driving . . . and I just double parked the car and jumped into the booth and did it really quickly."

Of course, Scott thought the whole thing was a total goof. "To tell you the truth, I don't know what I was thinking when I did that. I was going to a high school with a big drama program, but I was in the jock program," he told the *Calgary Sun*.

Imagine his surprise when he received a call from the Warner Brothers studio inviting him to audition for the part.

Of course, as everyone now knows, it was Chris O'Donnell who eventually slipped into Robin's tights. But a casting director at Warner Brothers saw Scott's tape and directed the young Canadian to a talent agent in Toronto.

The acting bug had bitten Scott Speedman— hard. There was no turning back from there.

Olympic Dreams

The youngest star on the WB's hit coming-of-age drama *Felicity* (he plays Ben Covington, the object of Felicity's first big crush) was born on September 1, 1975, in London, England. But before he could say "cheerio" (or develop an

English accent), Scott's family moved to Willowdale, Canada, a suburb of Toronto.

While Scott was growing up, acting was the furthest thing from his mind. He was a total jock—spending all of his time in the pool, swimming competitively. And we do mean competitively! Scott was such a natural that by the age of twelve he was chosen for a place on the Canadian Junior National Swim Team. Even more important, his coaches made no secret of the fact that if Scott worked hard enough, he was Olympic material.

Scott was in his mid-teens the first time he tried out at the Canadian Olympic swimming trials. He didn't place in that contest, but he was determined to work harder to make the team the next opportunity he had.

Unfortunately, fate sometimes has a way of changing your plans. And in Scott's case, fate came in the form of an injury to his neck and shoulder, which ended Scott's competitive swimming career.

Scott was completely lost. He had been swimming competitively all his life. Now here he was, in the middle of his high school career, with very little going for him. By his own admission, he was "never really a great student." And now, even his sporting days had been taken away from him.

But Scott isn't the kind of guy to let bad

things bring him down. He saw his injury as life's way of forcing him to change his priorities. He spent more time with his friends, and eventually established a steady relationship with the young lady who dared him to make that fateful plea on *Speaker's Forum*.

Early Acting Days

While he was starting out, Scott played it smart—he signed on for a few college courses at the University of Toronto.

The roles did not exactly come quickly. Scott went on a ton of auditions, but only found a few parts in TV shows filming in Toronto, including a guest shot on *Kung Fu: The Legend Continues*, a small part on an episode of *Goosebumps*, and a part Scott really despised—Nancy Drew's boyfriend, Ned, on the 1995 series *Nancy Drew*.

"It was the worst [role]," he recalled in *Us* magazine. "All [Ned] did was follow Nancy around, whining, 'C'mon, Nancy, we were supposed to go to the beach today.' "

And if Scott's acting roles weren't challenging enough for him, neither was school. He dropped out of the University of Toronto before the end of his freshman year.

Luckily, Scott didn't drop out of the acting biz, too. Because better roles were just around the corner.

Getting Noticed

In 1996, Scott found himself acting in some high-profile made-for-TV movies. He had a large role in *Giant Mine*, and worked opposite former Charlie's Angel Kate Jackson in *What Happened to Bobby Earl?* Although Scott was still not an actor whose name rolled off the tongues of casting directors, he *was* starting to make a name for himself, and eventually he found himself sharing the set with some Hollywood heavyweights on a made-for-TV movie called *Dead Silence*.

Dead Silence was a suspense thriller that starred Lolita Davidovich and Oscar winner Marlee Matlin. Scott was thrilled to be working with some big-name actors, and for the first time, he began to believe that he really was going to make it in the biz.

Shortly after he wrapped *Dead Silence*, Scott went to work on his first feature film—an independent movie called *Ursa Major*. The sci-fi love story can be summarized by the tag line on the movie's poster: "Life. Love. Glow-in-the-dark stars." It wasn't really Scott's idea of a quality film, but it was a chance to show what he could do on the big screen.

Scott's second independent feature was much more to his liking. In *Kitchen Party*, Scott played a troubled teen who had gathered up his friends to revolt against their traditional suburban middle-class upbringing.

"That's the one I'm really proud of," Scott says of his work in *Kitchen Party*. "I think it's a really good movie, and it's so fun to watch."

Now that Scott had established himself as an actor who could be trusted with roles in serious films, he decided it was time to take on a character that would allow him to really stretch his acting chops. That meant agreeing to play a character who was totally unlikable—an abusive boyfriend in the made-for-TV movie *Every 9 Seconds*.

It was soon after the filming of *Every 9 Seconds* that Scott's agent sent him a script for a TV series that would be shot in Los Angeles. The script was the pilot for *Felicity*. The show was about a girl named Felicity who suddenly decides to change all her life plans and dash across the country to New York City to be near a boy she has had a crush on all through high school. Scott's agent wanted his client to take a look at the character of Ben—a jock who had been a big fish in a small pond in his high school and was now trying to find his way at a university in New York City.

Becoming Ben

From the minute Scott read the *Felicity* pilot script, he knew he had to be part of this new TV series. "I think the original thing that attracted me to the show was its philosophy of following your heart," he told an on-line chat audience. "It's great to see this girl following her heart."

But flying to L.A. for the audition was out of the question—especially since the almost-broke Scott would have to pay for the flight. So he did the next best thing.

"I went to a casting house . . . where you pay fifty dollars for a half hour and recorded a videotape for my audition."

Scott had a feeling that most actors were going to focus on Ben's tough-jock exterior. But, being a sportsman himself, Scott knew that there is a lot more to athletes than their muscles. Just like anyone else, players have softer sides.

"I think most actors fell into the trap of playing [Ben] as the tough guy, not a guy with real heart. That's [the side of Ben] I *did* want to show," Scott explained to the *Calgary Sun*.

The producers must have liked what they saw on Scott's tape, because the next thing he knew, Scott was on a plane to L.A. to meet with the show's star, Keri Russell.

"A week after they received [the audition tape] they called up and said they wanted me based on the tape. It was a Wednesday. I flew down on Thursday, met Keri on Sunday, and we started shooting on Monday."

Life on the Set

It's not easy being part of a hit TV show. The actors on *Felicity* work fifteen- or sixteen-hour days sometimes, and then go home and fall into bed exhausted. On Friday nights, the cast doesn't leave the studio until 3:00 or 4:00 A.M. And while that can be draining, it helps that the five stars of the show—Keri Russell (Felicity), Scott Foley (Noel), Amy Jo Johnson (Julie), Tangi Miller (Elena), and Scott—are all good buddies who hang out together on and off the set.

While he's on the set and in between scenes, Scott likes to play basketball with the show's other hot Scott—Scott Foley. He also likes to walk around the lot.

"I can't sit in those trailers," he explains. "I like to watch what's going on or walk around. I walk a ton."

In fact, Scott wanders off the set so often that the crew presented him with a pager so they can find him whenever they need him.

On his few nights off, when he is not memorizing his lines, Scott likes to spend time with his *Felicity* family. As Keri Russell explains, "We hang out extracurricularly. Amy Jo plays guitar and sings at some local places. We all go and check it out."

Lately, however, Scott is finding that his

hanging-with-the-gang days are coming to an end. That's because he's in big demand in the film world. Last summer, while *Felicity* was on hiatus, Scott found himself in front of the cameras, starring opposite Hollywood's reigning queen, Gwyneth Paltrow, in *Duets*, a film directed by Gwyneth's father, Bruce Paltrow. As if playing opposite the 1999 Oscar winner wasn't enough pressure, Scott (and just about everyone else in the world) knew that the role of Billy the cab driver had originally been written for Gwyneth's former fiancé, Brad Pitt. And to make matters worse, the press was hinting that Scott had not only taken Brad's place in Gwyneth's film, he'd taken his place in her heart as well.

But Gwyneth and Scott have both made it perfectly clear that the two are friends. In fact, "Scott has become a good friend of the whole Paltrow family. Scott is like a little brother to [Gwyneth]," Gwyneth's publicity rep told reporters recently.

And Bruce Paltrow made sure that everyone knew he didn't want anyone else in the world to play Billy.

"Scott is very shy, very sweet, and very talented," he assured *USA Today*. And the director went on to tell *Entertainment Tonight* that the role required a "certain soulfulness" that Scott had "in spades."

In just a few short years, Scott went from being an unknown actor who was grateful to play a cop in a *Goosebumps* episode to a recognized talent starring in one of the most talked-about films of 1999. And yet, by all accounts, he was handling the pressures of stardom like a pro. How did he manage it? Well, according to Scott, it helps that his fans are really great people.

"The last thing I want to do is change my day-to-day life. I don't know if you ever really get used to it," he admits. "But it hasn't really been overwhelming. The fans are really sweet and friendly."

And all those fans have one question on their minds. How would Scott handle it if a girl he barely knew flew across the country to follow him?

"I'd be flattered," he admitted to *Jane* magazine. "Especially if she looked like Keri [Russell]. I mean, how bad could that be? What it comes down to is passion."

Better watch out, Scott. And get that guest room ready! Passion is exactly what you bring out in your millions of fans. But, girls, if you're smart, you'll stay home and watch Scott on TV. After all, with his busy schedule, *Felicity* may be the only place anyone will be able to spend a whole hour with Scott.

Fast Facts

Full name: Robert Scott Speedman
Birthday: September 1, 1975
Astrological sign: Virgo
Parents: Roy and Mary Speedman
Favorite book: *On the Road* by Jack Kerouac
Favorite colors: Blue and black
Favorite actor: Marlon Brando
Favorite clothes: Jeans and black T-shirts
Greatest fear: Sharks
Favorite sports: Swimming, basketball, tennis

Rider Strong
Boy No More!

In 1992, Rider Strong walked into a big audition with a lot of doubt in his mind. He was trying out for a part in a series that didn't even have a name yet—the title on the "sides" (the lines actors are given for auditions) read simply "Ben Savage Project."

Rider Strong was auditioning for the role of Shawn Hunter, best friend to the series' main character, Cory Matthews (who would be played by Ben Savage). Rider remembers feeling that he was totally wrong for the part.

"I remembering auditioning for the part of Shawn and thinking, 'I'm terrible for this part. I'm more of a Cory type. I'll never get it,'" he recalls.

But of course, Rider did get cast in the part of

Shawn, the sarcastic, wisecracking best buddy who was forever getting Cory in trouble.

In the beginning of the series, Rider didn't have a whole lot to do—he was only in two scenes during *Boy Meets World*'s September 1993 pilot episode—but soon the producers noticed that it was Shawn, and not Cory, who was making the show's viewers' hearts flutter. More and more air time was given to the character of Shawn.

That makes Rider's fans extremely happy. After all, as far as they are concerned, that original script should have been called "The Rider Strong Project" because it is Rider's strong, sexy good looks, impeccable timing, and intense sensitivity that draws them to their TV sets every Friday night.

Boy Meets Stage

Rider Strong is not exactly what you'd call your typical Los Angeles actor. In fact, he's not even from Los Angeles. Rider was born on December 11, 1979, in San Francisco, California. He grew up in a three-story log cabin his father built in a redwood forest outside of the city.

Rider's parents were totally into allowing their children to discover their creative sides. When they were growing up, Rider and his big brother, Shiloh, weren't even allowed to watch

TV. Ironically, it was that rule that eventually led Rider to becoming a TV star. Since they couldn't watch shows on TV, Rider and Shiloh wrote and performed their own shows, which they filmed on their dad's video camera. Acting and writing became his two passions.

"I kind of thank them for it now, but I hated it then," Rider recalls of his parents' no-TV rule.

Although he says he's a total nature boy at heart (and who wouldn't be, after growing up among trees, flowers, and wild animals?), Rider's early dreams were to perform on the stage—and a stage is hard to find in the middle of a redwood forest.

So when Rider was only nine years old, he started spending a lot of time in the city of San Francisco, playing the role of Gavroche in a production of the musical *Les Misérables*. (Because the show takes place in nineteenth-century France, Rider had to leave his hair long, which was the style of the day, and he recalls that "I always got mistaken for a girl." Can you imagine *anyone* mistaking red-hot Rider for a girl today?) Gavroche was not a huge role, but it did give Rider the chance to sing a solo on-stage—the big musical number "Little People." The inevitable applause that came each night at the end of the number was intoxicating, and from that moment on, Rider was hooked.

Eventually, Rider began taking day trips to

Los Angeles to audition for roles on TV and in the movies. In 1990, he got his first on-camera role, in an NBC movie of the week called *Long Road Home.* He had just one line—"I'm hungry." Still, Rider said doing the film was a learning experience—one that led to several more film roles, including a film called *Benefit of the Doubt,* in which he costarred with big-screen talents Amy Irving and Donald Sutherland.

Benefit of the Doubt was a big step for Rider. He was called upon to cry and bring intense emotions to the screen—not an easy task for an eleven-year-old kid. Rider was also involved in some scary speedboat chase scenes. But the action stuff wasn't the scariest part of being in the film. Rider says that watching Donald Sutherland play his psychotic grandfather "made me tremble during the filming of some scenes" because Sutherland was such a brilliant actor.

Amy Irving and Donald Sutherland were not the only huge stars Rider got to perform with during the early years of his career. He also got to spend some time with Mary Poppins herself—Julie Andrews—in her ABC sitcom *Julie.*

Rider remembers being thrilled to be cast as Julie's son in the series. After all, the network was very high on the show because of Julie Andrews's star status. Unfortunately, the show was not the hit the network had hoped for, and it was canceled after six episodes.

Still, Rider learned a lot from Julie—and not just about acting. He learned how to handle stardom with class.

"She was the nicest lady in the world," he remembers.

Rider didn't let the fall of the *Julie* sitcom hold him back. He just went on auditioning for new roles, and he scored quite a few of them. In the early 1990s, Rider could be seen guest-starring on series such as *Nurses, Home Improvement, Empty Nest, Time Trax,* and *Evening Shade.*

But it wasn't until he took on the role of *Boy Meets World's* Shawn Hunter that Rider Strong became a household name.

Meeting His New World

The first few weeks on a series are sort of like entering a new school. You don't know anyone, and no one knows you. It's hard to tell who your best friends are going to be. Rider and Ben Savage may have been cast as best friends, but their relationship didn't start out that way.

"Ben didn't like me that much," Rider tells fans who visit his Web site, looking back on the early days of the show. "He thought I was weird because I didn't play basketball."

Eventually, however, life began to imitate art, and Ben and Rider became as thick as Cory and

Shawn. "Now I hang out [with him] more than with any other actor I've ever worked with," Rider says. "He makes me smile more than anybody."

Rider was relieved to be working with kids his own age when he joined the cast of *Boy Meets World*. Before that, he'd usually been the only kid on the set, and that can get pretty lonely, especially for someone who takes his friendships as seriously as Rider.

To this day, Rider's closest friends are two guys he met back in elementary school—Indy and Nate. "I left their school when I got into acting," Rider says, "but I still keep in contact with them."

That's putting it mildly. Rider tries to go home to northern California as many weekends as possible during the year. And when he does take the four-hundred-mile trek, he usually spends the time hanging with Indy and Nate. "We do anything, just so we can hang out together," he told *Bop* magazine.

If Rider and Ben's rocky beginnings were completely different from the on-screen Shawn and Cory, so were the personalities of Rider and his character, Shawn. In fact, the two could not have been more different.

For starters, the two dressed differently. Shawn goes for bright, eye-catching colors, while in real life, Rider is more subdued in his look, going for jeans and hiking boots. And while both boys care deeply about their friends, in real life, Rider is far more up-front about his feelings than the ever-secretive Shawn will ever be. The character of Shawn is also not exactly what you might call a strong student. In fact, for several seasons, he didn't care about school at all. Rider, on the other hand, has always been a whiz when it comes to schoolwork. And he takes his education very seriously.

"School has always been easy for him," Rider's mom, Lin, told *Bop* magazine.

Rider is particularly strong in English. He reads almost constantly, and not just pulp fiction, either. He's into the classics by authors like John Steinbeck and Jack Kerouac. "I'm always in search of a good book," he claims.

Rider's also a fanatical writer who goes nowhere without his computer. And while Shawn might use a computer to play games, Rider uses his to write.

"I want to someday publish a book before I die," he vows. "That's my ultimate goal."

As the years have gone by, the writers on *Boy Meets World* have begun to integrate some of Rider's personality into Shawn's. Like Rider, Shawn now attends college, although for a while there was some doubt about whether he would ever go. And Shawn has also been revealed as a closet poetry freak—whose poems have been read at coffeehouses (even though it was Cory who did the actual reading). Rider himself has read some of his own poetry at local coffeehouses in L.A., and he hopes that through the character of Shawn he will be able to introduce his fans to the beauty of poetry.

Life Outside the *Boy Meets World* World

One thing Shawn has that Rider doesn't is a girl-friend. It's not that Rider wouldn't like a steady relationship, it's just that he doesn't have the time. Consider what his weekly work calendar looks like:

Friday: The cast of *Boy Meets World* sits at a table with the writers and directors and reads through the week's new script. Then the director begins blocking the scenes (working with the actors on where they should move during a scene).

Saturday and Sunday: Rider usually returns to northern California.

Monday: The actors must know their lines as they block out more scenes. That gets tough because the script changes from day to day.

Tuesday: There's more rehearsing and blocking of scenes.

Wednesday: The cast rehearses in front of the cameras.

Thursday: The cast arrives around noon and gets ready to tape the show that night in front of a live audience. ("That's the best part," Rider confides. "If we didn't tape in front of a live audience, it wouldn't be nearly as fun.")

And that's just Rider's *Boy Meets World* schedule. In 1996, Rider also took time to guest-star on a few episodes of the series *Party of Five*, opposite Lacey Chabert, as Claudia's boyfriend. A year later, he worked with his big bro, Shiloh, to direct and star in an antismoking educational video written by Shiloh called "Smokers and the People Who Smell Them." Then, in 1999, he guest-starred on two episodes of *The Practice* as Gary Ambrust, a teen who does not want to testify against his father—and winds up paying a heavy price.

As if all that career work weren't enough to keep Rider out of trouble, the brainy twenty-year-old is currently attending college out in California. Getting his degree is extremely important to Rider, even if it does take up what little free time he might have. "I've never been so busy in my life," he says of his school and work schedules.

What Does the Future Hold?

Rider may be too busy for a personal life at the moment, but he says he wouldn't trade his reality for anything. He's an optimist at heart, after all, and the way he sees it, being busy now means that he will be able to do the things he wants to later on in life. That includes penning some screenplays, and, of course, completing his novel.

"I like being an actor, but I want to eventually move into writing," he says.

He's already moving in that direction by working on a screenplay, *The Rain Kings*, and putting together a book of original poetry called *The Impulse*.

Rider would also like to make more movies, working both in front of and behind the cameras. "I want to tell my stories and of course surprise [the fans] with a reflection of reality," he says of his big-screen goals.

Those fans are never far from Rider's heart. No matter what career path Rider takes in the future, he says that he will never forget the people who have been watching him ever since *Boy Meets World* went on the air. In many ways, they've all grown up together, and Rider sees their well-being as a top priority in his life. That's why he's signed on as an ambassador for the Campaign for Tobacco-Free Kids, an organization dedicated to keeping kids from getting hooked on cigarettes.

Rider's favorite way of keeping in touch with his fans is through E-mail, and he checks his mailbox often. So if you have a question for him, that's the best place to reach him. Rider doesn't really like communicating by phone with people he hasn't met. Actually, Rider has a major case of phone phobia. "I have a fear of phones," he admitted to one magazine. "I can't think of any rational reason, except that I've had many embarrassing moments on the phone."

Some of those embarrassing moments come when fans search out his phone number and then call him as though they were old friends. The fans know who Rider is, but he doesn't have a clue who they might be. Rider has admitted to talking to kids on the phone for as long as ten minutes before realizing that he has no idea who is on the other end.

So here's a helpful hint: If you want to someday enter this boy's world, the best way to do it is through your modem.

Fast Facts

Full name: Rider King Strong
Nickname: Tavock
Birthday: December 11, 1979
Astrological sign: Sagittarius
Parents: Lin and King
Brother: Shiloh
Favorite Book: *East of Eden* and *Cannery Row* by John Steinbeck; *On the Road* by Jack Kerouac
Favorite food: French fries
Favorite actors: John Malkovich and Jack Nicholson
Hobbies: Reading, white-water rafting

The Super Sidekicks
Trivia Quiz

It's time to test your second-banana IQ. How much do you know about the sidekicks of TV, film, and the comics? There's only one way to find out. Take this Super Sidekicks Trivia Quiz.

Some of the questions are easy—they're taken from the latest and greatest shows and flicks around. But others are tougher—you'll have to be the kind of kid who's addicted to Nick at Nite and TV Land to get those right.

But don't let these questions about second bananas drive *you* bananas. If one stumps you, just tune in to pages 193–194. All the answers are there waiting for you.

1. On the old TV show *Rhoda*, Carlton, the doorman, was never seen. But his voice was

performed by Lorenzo Music. What cartoon cat did Lorenzo also speak for?

2. On *Seinfeld*, what was Newman's profession?

3. Name D. J. Tanner's best friend on *Full House*.

4. Name the Latin singing sensation who once had a supporting role in the Tom Berenger film *The Substitute*.

5. On *Sabrina, the Teenage Witch*, who is older, Zelda or Hilda?

6. *The Brady Bunch* was a huge sensation in the 1970s, and it lives on in reruns. In the series' last season, a cousin came to stay with the famed blended family. What was his name?

7. Which of *Titanic*'s supporting actors went on to romance the queen of the Nile in the TV miniseries *Cleopatra*?

8. All the friends on *Friends* are stars in their own right, but can you name Ross's sidekick from the show's early days? (Hint: He was a monkey.)

9. What *Happy Days* cast member started out as a bit player on the show only to become its leading man after fans latched on to his character?

10. What supporting actor on *7th Heaven* was also in the mega-hit action flick *Independence Day*?

11. Which of Gwyneth Paltrow's former real-life boyfriends had a supporting role in *Shakespeare in Love*?

12. *Titanic's* Leonardo DiCaprio had a supporting role in which Western?

13. Batman's sidekick, Robin, had another nickname. What was it?

14. On the classic 1950s sitcom *The Honeymooners*, what was the profession of Ralph's sidekick, Ed Norton?

15. What kiddie show did *Felicity's* Amy Jo Johnson star in?

16. Name the photographer at Superman's *Daily Planet* newspaper.

17. What rap sensation was once a sidekick on *Moesha?*

18. Who is Burky's R.A. on *Felicity?*

19. Before starring in *Sabrina, the Teenage Witch,* Melissa Joan Hart played the title character in another sitcom, *Clarissa Explains It All.* What was Clarissa's brother's name, and what nickname did Clarissa give him?

20. What *Gilligan's Island* sidekick served as a judge on *Say What! Karaoke* during MTV's "Isle of MTV" in 1999?

21. Name Drew Barrymore's third film, in which she played second banana to an alien.

22. What did *My So-Called Life's* Rayanne do to her best friend, Angela, to end their friendship?

23. In what film did Melissa Joan Hart take on a supporting role called simply Yearbook Girl?

24. Johnny Galecki, who played Max in *I Know What You Did Last Summer*, was the sidekick to which of Roseanne and Dan Conner's girls on *Roseanne?*

25. What Claire Danes' film featured Freddie Prinze, Jr., in a supporting role?

26. Name the gentleman's gentleman character who was the second banana to *Family Affair*'s Buffy and Jody.

27. On *I Love Lucy*, which two sidekicks owned the Ricardos' New York City apartment building?

28. The comic relief on the 1970s hit sitcom *Laverne & Shirley* (as if that funny show needed any more comedy!) were a duo of wacky neighbors named what?

29. The Lone Ranger was never really alone. He had a Native American sidekick. Name him.

30. Dynamo diva Madonna is usually a leading lady, but in this sporting movie, she was one of a whole team of sidekicks who played alongside Oscar winners Geena Davis and Tom Hanks. Name this home run–hitting film.

Answers to the Super Sidekicks Trivia Quiz

1. Garfield
2. A postman
3. Kimmy Gibbler

4. Marc Anthony
5. Zelda
6. Cousin Oliver
7. Billy Zane
8. Marcel
9. Henry Winkler's Fonzie
10. Andrew Keegan (Mary's boyfriend, Wilson)
11. Ben Affleck
12. *The Quick and the Dead*
13. The Boy Wonder
14. Sewer worker
15. *Mighty Morphin Power Rangers* (she was the pink ranger)
16. Jimmy Olsen
17. Usher
18. Felicity
19. Ferguson Darling, Ferg-face
20. Dawn Wells (who played Mary Ann)
21. *E.T.*
22. She had an affair with her boyfriend
23. *Can't Hardly Wait*
24. Darlene
25. *To Gillian on Her 37th Birthday*
26. Mr. French
27. Fred and Ethel Mertz
28. Lenny and Squiggy
29. Tonto
30. *A League of Their Own*

How Do You Measure Up?

25–30 correct: Take a bow! You've given an Oscar-winning performance (in the supporting players category, of course).

15–24 correct: Good job—you obviously know who the *real* stars are!

5–14 correct: Whoops! You've got some things to learn. Time to start staying up late and channel-surfing in search of old reruns.

0–5 correct: Yikes! Your score isn't as high as it could be. What happened? "You've got a lot of 'splaining to do" (as Lucy Ricardo's husband, Ricky, used to say on *I Love Lucy*).

About the Author

NANCY KRULIK is the author of more than one hundred books for children and young adults, including the *New York Times* bestsellers *Taylor Hanson: Totally Taylor!* and *Leonardo DiCaprio: A Biography*. She has also written biographies of pop stars Ricky Martin, JC Chasez, Isaac Hanson, and 98 Degrees, as well as the music trivia books *Pop Quiz* and *Pop Quiz: Country Music*. She lives in Manhattan with her husband, composer Daniel Burwasser, and their two children.

In time of tragedy,
a love that would not die...

Hindenburg, 1937
By Cameron Dokey

San Francisco Earthquake, 1906
By Kathleen Duey

Chicago Fire, 1871
By Elizabeth Massie

Washington Avalanche, 1910
By Cameron Dokey

---

sweeping stories of star-crossed romance

Starting in July 1999

From Archway Paperbacks
Published by Pocket Books

At a time when most kids
are trying to figure out who they are,
they're trying to figure out WHAT they are.

ROSWELL HIGH™

*Where school is an entirely
different experience...*

**Read the books that started it all
and watch ROSWELL™ this fall on the WB**

POCKET
PULSE

Published by Pocket Books

™ & © 1999 by Pocket Books. All Rights Reserved